Superfudge

Superfudge

by Judy Blume

A YEARLING BOOK

Published by
Dell Publishing Co., Inc.
1 Dag Hammarskjold Plaza
New York, New York 10017

Yearling ® TM 913705, Dell Publishing Co., Inc.

ISBN: 0-440-78433-6

Reprinted by arrangement with E.P. Dutton, a division of
Elsevier-Dutton Publishing Company, Inc.

Printed in the United States of America

Book Club Edition

August 1982

20 19 18 17 16 15 14

WFH

The author and publisher gratefully acknowledge permission to reprint the quoted passages on:

pages 78 and 79, from "Toot, Toot, Tootsie! Good-bye" by Gus Kahn, Ernie Erdman and Ted Fiorito. Copyright © 1922, renewed 1950 Leo Feist, Inc. All rights reserved. Used by permission.

page 90, from *One fish two fish red fish blue fish* by Dr. Seuss. ©Copyright, 1960, by Dr. Seuss. Published in New York by Beginner Books, Inc., a Division of Random House, Inc.

page 90, from *Green Eggs and Ham* by Dr. Seuss. ©Copyright 1960, by Dr. Seuss. Published in New York by Beginner Books, Inc., a Division of Random House, Inc.

pages 121 and 122, from the Superman property. The two quotes are from the Superman property and are trademarks of DC Comics Inc. © 1938. Used with permission.

page 130, from "Santa Claus Is Comin' To Town," words by Haven Gillespie and music by J. Fred Coots. Copyright © 1934, renewed 1962 Leo Feist, Inc. All rights reserved. Used by permission.

for Larry,
without whom there would be no Fudge

and for all my readers who have asked for
another book about him

Contents

1

Guess What, Peter?

Life was going along okay when my mother and father dropped the news. *Bam!* Just like that.

"We have something wonderful to tell you, Peter," Mom said before dinner. She was slicing carrots into the salad bowl. I grabbed one.

"What is it?" I asked. I figured maybe my father's been made president of the company. Or maybe my teacher phoned, saying that even though I don't get the best grades in the fifth grade, I am definitely the smartest kid in the class.

"We're going to have a baby," Mom said.

"We're going to what?" I asked, starting to choke. Dad had to whack me on the back. Tiny pieces of chewed up carrot flew out of my mouth and hit the counter. Mom wiped them up with a sponge.

"Have a baby," Dad said.

"You mean you're pregnant?" I asked Mom.

"That's right," she told me, patting her middle. "Almost four months."

"Four months! You've known for four months and you didn't tell me?"

"We wanted to be sure," Dad said.

"It took you four months to be sure?"

"I saw the doctor for the second time today," Mom said. "The baby's due in February." She reached over and tried to tousle my hair. I ducked and got out of the way before she could touch me.

Dad took the lid off the pot on the stove and stirred up the stew. Mom went back to slicing carrots. You'd have thought we were discussing the weather.

"How could you?" I shouted. "*How could you?* Isn't one enough?"

They both stopped and looked at me.

I kept right on shouting. "Another Fudge! Just what this family needs." I turned and stormed down the hall.

Fudge, my four-year-old brother, was in the living room. He was shoving crackers into his mouth and laughing like a loon at *Sesame Street* on TV. I looked at him and thought about having to go through it all over again. The kicking and the screaming and the messes and more—much more. I felt so angry that I kicked the wall.

Fudge turned. "Hi, Pee-tah," he said.

"You are the biggest pain ever invented!" I yelled.

He tossed a handful of crackers at me.

I raced to my room and slammed the door, so hard my map of the world fell off the wall and landed on the bed. My dog, Turtle, barked. I opened the door just enough to let him squeeze through, then slammed it shut again. I pulled my Adidas bag out of the closet and emptied two dresser drawers into it. *Another Fudge*, I said to myself. *They're going to have another Fudge*.

There was a knock at my door, and Dad called, "Peter . . ."

"Go away," I told him.

"I'd like to talk to you," he said.

"About what?" As if I didn't know.

"The baby."

"What baby?"

"You *know* what baby!"

"We don't need another baby."

"Need it or not, it's coming," Dad said. "So you might as well get used to the idea."

"Never!"

"We'll talk about it later," Dad said. "In the meantime, scrub up. It's time for dinner."

"I'm not hungry."

I zipped up my bag, grabbed a jacket and opened my bedroom door. No one was there. I marched down the hall and found my parents in the kitchen.

"I'm leaving," I announced. "I'm not going to hang around waiting for another Fudge to get born. Goodbye."

I didn't move. I just stood there, waiting to see what they'd do next.

"Where are you going?" Mom asked. She took four plates out of the cabinet and handed them to Dad.

"To Jimmy Fargo's," I said, although until that moment I hadn't thought at all about where I would go.

"They have a one-bedroom apartment," Mom said. "You'd be very crowded."

"Then I'll go to Grandma's. She'll be happy to have me."

"Grandma's in Boston for the week, visiting Aunt Linda."

"Oh."

"So why don't you scrub up and have your dinner, and then you can decide where to go," Mom said.

I didn't want to admit that I was hungry, but I was. And all those good smells coming from the pots and pans on the stove were making my mouth water. So I dropped my Adidas bag and went down the hall to the bathroom.

Fudge was at the sink. He stood on his stool, lathering his hands with three inches of suds. "Hello, you must be Bert," he said in his best *Sesame Street* voice. "My name is Ernie. Glad to meet you." He offered me one of his sudsy little hands.

"Roll up your sleeves," I told him. "You're making a mess."

"Mess, mess . . . I love to make a mess," he sang.

"We know . . . we know," I told him.

I ran my hands under the faucet and dried them on my jeans.

When we got to the table, Fudge arranged himself in his chair. Since he refuses to sit in his booster seat, he has to kneel so that he can reach his place at the table. "Pee-tah didn't scrub," he said. "He only rinsed."

"You little . . ." I started to say, but Fudge was already yapping away to my father.

"Hello, I'm Bert. You must be Ernie."

"That's right," my father said, playing along with him. "How are you, Bert?"

"Well, I'll tell you," Fudge said. "My liver's turning green and my toenails are falling off."

"Sorry to hear that, Bert," my father said. "Maybe tomorrow will be a better day."

"Yes, maybe," Fudge said.

I shook my head and piled some mashed potatoes on my plate. Then I drowned them in gravy. "Remember when we took Fudge to Hamburger Heaven," I said, "and he smeared the mashed potatoes all over the wall?"

"I did that?" Fudge asked, suddenly interested.

"Yes," I told him, "and you dumped a plate of peas on your head too."

My mother started to laugh. "I'd forgotten all about that day."

"Too bad you didn't remember before you decided to have *another* baby," I said.

"Baby?" Fudge asked.

My mother and father looked at each other. I got the message. They hadn't told Fudge the good news yet.

"Yes," Mom said. "We're going to have a baby."

"Tomorrow?" Fudge asked.

"No, not tomorrow," Mom said.

"When?" Fudge asked.

"February," Dad said.

"January, February, March, April, May, June, July . . ." Fudge recited.

"Okay . . . okay . . ." I said. "We all know how smart you are."

"Ten, twenty, thirty, forty, fifty . . ."

"Enough!" I said.

"A, B, C, D, E, F, G, R, B, Y, Z . . ."

"Will somebody turn him off?" I said.

Fudge was quiet for a few minutes. Then he said, "What kind of new baby will it be?"

"Let's hope it's not like you," I said.

"Why not? I was a good baby, wasn't I, Mommy?"

"You were an interesting baby, Fudgie," Mom said.

"See, I was an interesting baby," he said to me.

"And Peter was a sweet baby," Mom said. "He was very quiet."

"Lucky you had me first," I said to Mom, "or you might not have had any more kids."

"Was I a quiet baby, too?" Fudge asked.

"I wouldn't say that," Dad said.

"I want to see the baby," Fudge said.

"You will."

"Now!"

"You can't see it now," Dad said.

"Why not?" Fudge asked.

"Because it's inside me," Mom told him.

Here it comes, I thought, *the big question*. When I asked it, I got a book called *How Babies Are Made*. I wondered what Mom and Dad would say to Fudge. But Fudge didn't ask. Instead, he banged his spoon against his plate and howled. "I want to see the baby. I want to see the baby now!"

"You'll have to wait until February," Dad said, "just like the rest of us."

"Now now now!" Fudge screamed.

Another five years of this, I thought. *Maybe even more. And who's to say that they aren't going to keep on having babies, one after the other.* "Excuse me," I said, getting up from the table. I went into the kitchen and grabbed my Adidas bag. Then I stood in the doorway and called, "Well, I'd better be on my way." I sort of waved good-bye.

"Where is Pee-tah going?" Fudge asked.

"I'm running away," I told him. "But I'll come back to visit. Someday."

"No, Pee-tah . . . don't go!" Fudge jumped off his chair and ran to me. He grabbed my leg and started bawling. "Pee-tah . . . Pee-tah . . . take me with you."

I tried to shake him off my leg but I couldn't. He can be really strong. I looked at my mother and father. Then I looked down at Fudge, who gave me the same look as Turtle when he's begging for a biscuit. "If only I knew for sure what the baby would be like," I said.

"Take a chance, Peter," Dad said. "The baby won't necessarily be anything like Fudge."

"But it won't necessarily *not* be like him either," I answered.

Fudge tugged at my leg. "I want an interesting baby," he said. "Like me."

I sighed. "If you think it's going to sleep in *my* room, you're crazy," I told Mom and Dad.

"The baby will sleep in here," Mom said. "In the dining area."

"Then where will we eat?"

"Oh, we'll think of something," Mom said.

I put my Adidas bag down and tried shaking

Fudge off one more time. "Okay," I said, "I'll stay for now. But when the baby comes, if I don't like it, I'm leaving."

"Me too," Fudge said. "Sam got a new baby and it smells." He held his nose. "P.U."

"Who wants dessert?" Dad asked. "It's vanilla pudding."

"I do . . . I do . . ." Fudge yelped. He let go of me and climbed into his chair.

"Peter?" Dad said.

"Sure, why not?" And I sat down at the table too.

Mom reached over and tousled my hair. This time I let her.

2

Cutchie-Cutchie-Coo

Before the end of the week, Fudge asked the big question. "How did the baby get inside you, Mommy?" So Mom borrowed my copy of *How Babies Are Made*, and she read it to Fudge.

As soon as he had the facts straight, he was telling anybody and everybody exactly how Mom and Dad had made the baby. He told Henry, our elevator operator. Henry smiled and said, "That's a mouthful for a small fry like you."

He told the checker at the supermarket. Her eyes got bigger and bigger until Mom said, "That's enough, Fudgie."

"But I'm just getting to the good part," Fudge said.

"Peter," Mom said, "it's getting very warm in here. Why don't you take Fudge outside?"

He saw a pregnant woman on the bus and said, "I know what's growing inside you, and I know how it got there too." The woman got up and changed her seat.

He told Grandma. She said to my mother, "Anne, do you think it's wise for him to know *so* much? In my days we talked about the stork."

"What's a stork?" Fudge asked.

"It's a big bird," I told him.

"Like Big Bird on *Sesame Street*?"

"Not exactly."

"I like birds," Fudge said. "I want to be one when I grow up."

"You can't be a bird," Grandma said.

"Why not?"

"Because you're a boy."

"So what?" Fudge said, and he laughed like crazy and turned somersaults on the floor.

Fudge never stopped talking about his favorite subject. He told his nursery school class, and his teacher was so impressed she phoned and asked Mom to come to school. The children had a lot of questions for her. So Mom went to Fudge's class and enjoyed it so much she offered to come to my class too. I told her, "No thanks!"

I hadn't told anyone she was going to have a baby, except Jimmy Fargo. I tell him just about everything.

And Sheila Tubman knew, because she lives in our building and could see that Mom was pregnant.

"She's very old to be having a baby, isn't she?" Sheila asked one afternoon.

"She's thirty-four," I said.

Sheila opened her mouth. "Oh, she's *really* old!"

"She's not as old as your mother," I said. I had no idea how old Mrs. Tubman was, but Sheila's sister, Libby, was thirteen, so I guessed that Mrs. Tubman was older than Mom.

"But you don't see *my* mother having a baby, do you?" Sheila asked.

"No . . . but . . ." I couldn't think of anything else to say. I didn't understand what she was getting at anyway.

When I went upstairs I asked Mom, "Isn't thirty-four old to be having a baby?"

"I don't think so," Mom said. "Why?"

"Just wondering."

"Grandma had Aunt Linda when she was thirty-eight."

"Oh." So my mother wasn't the oldest woman in the world to be having a baby. And Sheila didn't know what she was talking about, as usual.

o   o   o   o

On February 26, while my fifth grade class was on a trip to the Metropolitan Museum of Art, my sister was born. Later I found out that she was born at exactly 2:04 in the afternoon, just as we were in the Egyptian Room, studying the mummies.

They named her Tamara Roxanne, but for weeks everybody called her The Baby. "The Baby is crying." "The Baby is hungry." "Shush. . . . The Baby is sleeping."

Soon, instead of calling her The Baby, Mom started saying dumb things, like "How's my little Tootsie-Wootsie?" as if The Baby could answer her. "Does my little Tootsie-Wootsie need to be changed?" Yes, almost always! "Does my little Tootsie-Wootsie need a feeding?" Yes, almost always!

And Mom's little Tootsie-Wootsie never slept more than two hours at a time. Every night I'd wake up to her howls. Turtle, who slept at the foot of my bed, woke up too. Then he'd howl along with her. A regular duet!

o   o   o   o

By the time she was one month old, everybody was calling her Tootsie. Right away I could see that there would be problems. I tried to warn my mother and father. "When she goes to school with a name like that, the kids are going to tease her. They'll call her Tootsie Roll. Or worse!"

Mom and Dad just laughed. "Oh Peter, you're so funny."

Only I wasn't being funny at all. I knew what I was talking about. But there was nothing I could do

13

about it. I had a brother called Fudge. And now I had a sister called Tootsie. Maybe what my parents really wanted was a candy factory. I wondered how come I got off so easy.

Tootsie was much smaller than I'd expected, but she was tough. I found that out when Fudge tried to pull off her toes. "I just wanted to see what would happen," he explained when Tootsie screamed.

"You must *never* do that again!" Mom told him. "How would you like it if Peter tried to pull off your toes?"

I couldn't help laughing at that one.

"Peter knows my toes don't come off," Fudge said.

"Well, neither do Tootsie's!" Mom said.

o o o o

One afternoon when I came home from school, Tootsie wasn't in her crib. I figured Mom was feeding her, so I went to her bedroom to say hello. Mom was lying on her bed with her hands over her eyes. "Hi," I said. "Where's Tootsie?"

"In her crib, asleep," Mom muttered.

"No, she's not."

"Of course she is. I just put her down a few minutes ago."

"I looked in her crib and I'm telling you, she's not there."

Mom took her hands away from her face. "What are you saying, Peter?"

"Mom, Tootsie's not in her crib. That's all I'm saying."

Mom jumped up. "Then where is she?"

We both ran down the hall and into the area where we used to eat. Mom looked into her crib but Tootsie wasn't there.

"Oh, no!" Mom cried. "She's been kidnapped."

"Who'd want her?" As soon as I said it, I was sorry.

"Call the police, Peter . . ." Mom said. "No, wait, call Dad first . . . no, call the police . . . dial 911. . . ."

"Wait a minute, Mom," I said. "Where's Fudge?"

"Fudge? In his room, I guess. He was listening to records when I put Tootsie down for a nap." She looked thoughtful for a minute. "You don't think . . ."

We raced down to Fudge's room. He was sitting on the floor playing with his Matchbox cars and listening to "Puff the Magic Dragon" on his record player.

"Where's Tootsie?" Mom said.

"Tootsie?" Fudge asked, sounding a lot like me when I'm trying to get out of answering a question.

"Yes, Tootsie!" Mom said, louder.

"She's hiding," Fudge said.

"What are you talking about?"

"We're playing a game," Fudge told her.

"Who's playing a game?" Mom asked.

"Us," Fudge said. "Me and Tootsie."

"Tootsie can't play. She's too young for games."

"I help her," Fudge said. "I help her hide."

"Fudge," Mom said, and I could tell that in another minute she'd really let him have it, "where is Tootsie?"

"I can't tell. She'll be mad."

Just as my mother was about to explode, I had an idea. "Let's play Hot and Cold," I said to Fudge. "You follow me, and when I get close to Tootsie, you say *hot*; and when I get far away from her, you say *cold*. Get it?"

"I like games," Fudge said.

"Okay . . . ready?"

"Ready."

"Let's go." I walked down the hall to the living room.

"Cold . . . cold . . . cold . . ." Fudge sang.

I went into the kitchen. "Cold . . . cold . . . cold."

I walked into the front hall.

"Hot . . . oh, hot!" Fudge cried.

I opened the guest closet.

"Very hot . . . watch out, you'll get burned." He jumped up and down, clapping his hands.

Tootsie was on the floor of the closet, fast asleep in her infant seat. Mom scooped her up in her arms. "Oh, thank goodness, my little Tootsie-Wootsie is all right!" Mom put her back into her crib. And then she really let go. "That was a very naughty thing to do," she shouted. "I'm very angry at you, Fudge."

"But Tootsie likes to play."

"Have you hidden her before?"

"Yes."

"You must *never* do that again. Do you understand?"

"No."

"You can't carry her around that way."

"She's not heavy."

"But babies have to be carried in a special way."

"You mean like mother cats carry their kittens?" Fudge asked.

"That's right," Mom told him.

Fudge laughed. "But you don't carry Tootsie in your mouth."

"No, I don't. But I do carry her very carefully, to protect her."

"Do you love me, Mommy?"

"Yes, very much."

"Then get rid of Tootsie," Fudge said. "I'm sick of her. She's no fun."

"Someday she'll be fun. And she'll be able to play Hide-and-Seek with you. But you have to wait. She's not ready yet."

"I don't want to wait. I want you to get rid of her. Now!"

"Tootsie is our baby. . . ."

"I'm your baby!"

"You're my little boy."

"No, I'm your baby."

"All right," Mom said, "you're my baby, too."

"Then pick me up, like you do Tootsie."

Mom opened her arms and Fudge jumped up into them. He rested his head on Mom's shoulder, shoved his fingers into his mouth, and slurped on them.

I know it's stupid, but just for a minute I wished I could be Mom's baby again, too.

o   o   o   o

After that, whenever we had company, Fudge tried to sell Tootsie. "You like the baby?" he'd ask.

"Oh, yes . . . she's just adorable."

"You can have her for a quarter."

When that didn't work, he tried to give her away. "We have a baby upstairs and you can have her for free," he'd say to anyone on the street.

When that didn't work, he tried to *pay* to have someone *take* her away. "I'll give you a quarter if you take her to your house and never bring her back."

He tried that with Sheila Tubman.

"My mother told me when I was born, Libby wanted to get rid of me, too," Sheila said.

Who could blame her? I thought.

"But she got over it and so will you," she told Fudge.

Fudge kicked Sheila. Then he ran down the hall.

Sheila stood over Tootsie's crib. "Lucky for her, she doesn't look like you, Peter."

"What's that supposed to mean?" I said.

"Look in the mirror sometime. Cutchie-cutchie-coo . . ." she said to Tootsie.

"We talk to her like she's a regular person," I said.

"But she's not a regular person," Sheila told me. "She's a baby."

"So . . . you don't have to make those stupid noises at her."

"But she likes them. Watch this . . . if I tickle her under her chin, she smiles."

"It just looks like she's smiling, but really, it's gas."

"Oh no . . . Tootsie is smiling just for me, aren't you, you precious little thing?"

It did look like Tootsie was smiling. But why would anybody smile at Sheila Tubman, even a baby?

That night, Fudge climbed into Tootsie's crib. "I'm the baby," he said. "Ga ga ga."

Dad lifted him out of the crib. "You're a big boy. You sleep in a big-boy bed."

"No, I'm not a big boy. I'm a baby. Waa waa waa. . . ."

I decided it was time to have a little talk with the kid. So I said, "Hey, Fudge . . . you want me to read you a story?"

"Yes."

"Okay . . . get into bed and I'll be right there."

I brushed my teeth and put on my pajamas. When I got to Fudge's room, he was sitting up in bed with his favorite book spread out across his lap. *Arthur the Anteater*. "Read," he said.

I sat down next to him. "Aren't you tired of acting like a baby?" I asked.

"No."

"I thought you wanted to be like me."

"I do."

"Well, you can't be a baby and be like me, too."

"Why not?"

"Uh . . . because babies can't do anything. They just eat and sleep and cry. They aren't even interesting."

"Then why does everybody think Tootsie's so great?"

"Because she's new. They'll get tired of her pretty soon. It's better to be older."

"Why?"

"We get more privileges."

"What's *privileges*?"

"It means we get to do things she can't do."

"Like what?"

"Like staying up late and uh . . . watching TV . . . and all sorts of things."

"I don't get to stay up late. *You* do."

"That's because I'm the biggest brother. But you'll get to stay up later than Tootsie."

"When?"

"When she's four and you're eight. Then you'll get to stay up a lot later. And you'll go to school, and you'll know how to read and write, and she won't. And uh . . ."

"Read," Fudge said, sliding down under the covers.

"Will you stop trying to be a baby?" I asked.

"I'll think about it."

"Well, that's better than nothing," I said.

Fudge fell asleep before I'd finished the book. I pulled up his covers and turned out his light. Then I went into the bathroom and studied myself in the mirror. What was Sheila Tubman talking about? I looked the same as always. And why did she think Tootsie was lucky not to look like me? Unless it was my ears. Lately, they seemed too big. I tried holding them flat against the side of my head. *Not bad*, I thought. *Maybe I could tape them back every morning before school. But that would be a lot of trouble. If I grew my hair longer I could hide them. Yes, that's what I'd do. Grow my hair until it covered my ears.* I yawned. When I yawn while I'm looking in the mirror, I can see my tonsils.

I went to my room, got into bed, and fell asleep. Who cared what Sheila Tubman thought, anyway!

3

Another Something Wonderful

Life at our house had definitely changed. Dad would come home at night with an armful of grocery bags and fix our dinner. The washing machine was always running. Every time Tootsie had a feeding and was burped, she'd spit up. She had to be changed about six times a day. Fudge started wetting his pants again, and then his bed. Mom and Dad said he was just going through a phase and that if we were patient, it would pass. I suggested putting him back in diapers but nobody else thought that was a very good idea.

One afternoon, Mom started to cry. Right in front of me. "What's wrong?" I asked.

"I'm just so tired," she said. "There's so much to do. Sometimes I think I won't be able to make it through the week."

"That's what you get for having another baby!" I told her.

That only made her cry harder. I don't like to see my mother cry. I feel sorry for her, but at the same time she makes me angry.

Grandma came over a few days a week to help. And Mom hired Libby Tubman to take care of Fudge after school. I stayed at Jimmy Fargo's until dinnertime. Nobody seemed to miss me around the house, anyway.

o   o   o   o

By the middle of May, life had improved. Tootsie was sleeping four hours at a clip during the day, and even longer at night. Dad and Mom were fixing dinner together. And Mom talked about going back to college to get a degree in art history, which surprised me. Because before I was born, she worked as a dental assistant.

"Why art history?" I asked.

"Because it interests me," she said.

"What about teeth? Aren't you interested in teeth anymore?"

"Well, yes," Mom said. "But not as much as art history. I think I'm ready for a change."

"Isn't having Tootsie enough of a change?"

"Yes, but someday she'll grow up and go to school, and I'll want to have a career."

"Oh," I said, not sure that I really understood.

o   o   o   o

On the last day of school we had a class party, with cupcakes and Island Punch. I drank eight cups of it. Island Punch is my favorite drink. Mom says I'm addicted to it. And I tell her, "That's right. If you cut me open, you'll find seven natural fruit flavors running through my veins." After drinking eight cups in a row, then riding home on the bus, then walking to my building, then waiting for the elevator, then dashing down the hall to our apartment, then digging out the key and unlocking the door, I really had to use the bathroom. I mean, *really*.

But Fudge was already in there, sitting on the toilet, turning the pages of *Arthur the Anteater*.

"Hurry up," I told him. "I've got to go."

"It's not good for me to hurry," Fudge said.

So I ran to Mom's room, but the door to her bathroom was locked. "Mom . . ." I called, banging on the door.

"Can't hear you . . ." she called back. "The shower's running. I'll be out in five minutes. Check on Tootsie, would you?"

So I ran back to my bathroom but Fudge hadn't moved. "Come on," I said. "This is an emergency. I drank eight cups of Island Punch this afternoon."

"I drank two glasses of Choco."

"How about getting off for just a minute?"

"It wouldn't be good for me," he said.

"Come on, Fudge!"

"I can't *think* when you're in here," he said.

"What do you have to think about?"

"Making!"

I could have lifted him off. But now that he's stopped wetting, we're all supposed to encourage him to use the toilet. So I ran down the hall again, thinking Tootsie has it easy. She just lets it out wherever and whenever.

Then I remembered that my teacher had read us a book about life in England in the eighteenth century. People used chamber pots instead of toilets way back then. I wished we had an old chamber pot handy. I was getting desperate. I ran into the living room and looked around. We have a big plant over in the corner. It stands more than five feet high. *Should I?* I wondered. *No, that's disgusting!* I thought. *But when you've got to go, you've got to go*, I reminded myself. I loosened my belt buckle.

As I did, Fudge called, "Okay, Pee-tah . . . I'm done. You do the flush."

Fudge refuses to flush the toilet. He's afraid he'll go down the drain too. But this wasn't the time to try to convince him he was wrong. I raced down the hall and relieved myself. Fudge watched. He was really impressed. "I never saw so much at once," he said.

"Thanks," I told him.

o   o   o   o

That night we were all sitting around in the living room, watching TV. I was holding Tootsie on my lap. She let out a soft little sigh. She's a lot like Turtle when he's asleep. I can tell what kind of dream he's having by the noises he makes. And sometimes, when he's having a nightmare, he cries out and shakes. Then I pet him until he's calm again.

It's the same with Tootsie. She'll be fast asleep, but she'll make these little noises or cry out and wiggle around. Other times, she'll work her mouth just like she's sucking on her bottle. I guess she dreams about eating a lot. But the little sighs are my favorites, because then I know she's content. And she feels so warm and soft, lying in my arms that way, that I feel good all over.

As soon as the show was over, Dad snapped off the TV, turned to face us, and said, "We have some really good news for you, boys."

"Oh no, not again," I said, looking down at Tootsie.

Mom and Dad laughed. "Something different, this time," Dad said.

"Is it interesting?" Fudge asked, racing his little

cars across the floor, "Vrooom . . . vrooom . . . vrooom. . . ."

"Yes, very interesting," Mom said.

"Well, don't keep us in suspense," I said. "Let's hear it."

"Is *suspense* like *privilege?*" Fudge asked.

"No," I told him. "Now shut up and listen." I looked at my father. "Well?" I asked. Because their idea of something interesting and my idea of something interesting aren't necessarily the same.

"We're moving to Princeton," Dad said.

"We're what?" I wanted to jump up but I couldn't. Not with Tootsie on my lap.

"Is Princeton near the park?" Fudge asked, running his little red car up and down Mom's leg.

"No, stupid," I said. "It's in New Jersey."

"Is New Jersey near the park?" he asked.

"Not Central Park," Mom said.

"But you won't need Central Park," Dad said. "Because you'll have your own backyard."

"What's a backyard?" Fudge asked.

"It's like a small park," Mom told him.

"My own park?" Fudge asked.

"More or less," Dad said, to shut him up.

"What about art history?" I said to Mom.

"What about it?" she answered.

"I thought you were going to go back to school to study art history."

"Princeton University has an art history department. I may take classes there."

"It's just for a year," Dad said, looking at me. "To see how we like being away from the city."

"Away . . . away . . . away . . ." Fudge sang. You can't have a conversation in front of him. It's useless. Couldn't my mother and father see that?

"We're going next week," Dad said.

"What about Maine?" I asked. We always go to Maine for two weeks in the summer.

"*M-a-i-n-e* spells *Maine*," Fudge sang. "*M-a-i-n-e*."

"How does he know how to spell *Maine*?" Mom asked Dad.

"I've no idea," Dad said.

"So what about it?" I pressed. "Are we going to Maine?"

"We're going to Princeton instead," Dad told me.

"Instead . . . instead . . . instead . . ." Fudge babbled.

"Shut up!" I yelled at him. And then I said just as loud, "I hate Princeton!"

"You've never even been there," Mom said.

"Oh, yes I have. We went to visit some dumb friends of yours, and they served us this disgusting dinner . . . shrimp and mushrooms and spinach all mixed together. And I was hungry but they wouldn't give me anything else to eat. Not even an extra piece of bread . . . I remember. . . ."

"Oh, that's right," Mom said. "I'd forgotten all about that day at Millie and George's house."

"You forget everything that's important!"

"Look, Peter," Dad said. "We were hoping you'd be pleased about Princeton. We've already rented a house there. In fact, we've rented Millie and George's house. They're going to Europe for the year."

"That old dump!"

"It's not a dump. It's a beautiful old place. And we've arranged to sublet our apartment. So I'd like you to keep an open mind about this."

"Open . . . open . . . open . . ." Fudge sang.

"You should have told me before. Just like you should have told me about Tootsie as soon as you knew. You never tell me anything. And here," I said, shoving Tootsie at Dad. "Why don't you hold your stupid baby yourself . . . because I have things to do." I got up and marched across the living room, kicking a couple of Fudge's cars as I went. By the time I got to my room, he was crying. *Good*, I thought.

And then Tootsie started. *Better yet!*

And then Turtle began to bark. *Let them suffer!*

I slammed my bedroom door, and my map wound up on my bed again.

o   o   o   o

I guess I fell asleep in my clothes, because next thing I knew Mom was shaking me and saying,

"Come on, Peter . . . get undressed and under the covers. It's late."

"Too hot for covers . . ." I mumbled.

"Okay . . . if you want to sleep in your clothes tonight, you can. But at least take off your sneakers."

". . . like them where they are," I said, sleepily.

"Okay. If you want to sleep in your sneakers, just for tonight . . ."

"Maybe every night . . ."

Mom ignored that. "Peter . . . about Princeton," she began.

I held up my hand. "Don't want to talk about it."

"You don't have to talk. Just listen."

"Too tired to listen."

"All right. We'll talk about it tomorrow."

"Anyway, nothing I can do about it . . . just like Tootsie . . . nothing I could do about her either."

"But you don't mind her now, do you?"

"Getting used to her."

"And you'll get used to Princeton, too. You'll see."

Then she started telling me about where I'd go to school, but I was still half-asleep and not really listening until she said something like . . . *having your little brother in the same school.*

And I sat up, suddenly wide-awake. "What did you say?"

"About what?"

"Just now . . . about Fudge and school?"

"Oh . . . we've had him tested. And even though

he's a little young, we're going to be able to enroll him in kindergarten. After all, he's had a full year of nursery school, and you know he can count by tens and recite the alphabet, and he knows his months and days of the week and colors, and . . . he can even spell *Maine*."

"Yeah . . . yeah . . ." I said. "We all know the kid's a genius. But you said something else . . . about him going to the same school as me?"

"That's right. You'll be in sixth grade and he'll be in kindergarten. Won't that be fun?"

"Fun!" That did it. I jumped off the bed and grabbed my Adidas bag. "You think it's fun to go to a new school? I don't even know anybody there. And I definitely don't want to go to school with the little monster. You don't understand anything, do you?" I opened my dresser drawers and dumped my clothes into the bag. "This time I'm *really* leaving!"

"Peter, honey . . ." Mom said. "You can't run away every time you hear something you think you don't like."

"I don't *think* it, I *know* it!"

"Even so, running away doesn't solve anything."

"Maybe not for you . . . but it does for me." I tossed in my baseball glove, my favorite jeans, half of my *Mad* magazines, a few of my smaller maps and a couple of tapes.

"Shall I make you a peanut butter sandwich to take along?" Mom asked, smiling.

"Don't give me any of that little boy stuff!" I told her. "Because I mean it . . . I'm leaving!"

She stopped smiling. "I can understand how you feel . . . but Daddy and I thought . . ."

"Daddy and you don't think the same way as me."

"I'm beginning to see that."

"And if you cared about me at all . . . even just a little bit . . . you wouldn't have done this. You wouldn't have!"

"Peter, we care about you a lot. That's one of the reasons for moving to Princeton. And we didn't even get to tell you the really big news."

"Oh, there's more?" I said. "Well, I can't wait to hear it."

"Daddy is taking the year off."

I stopped packing. "He quit his job at the agency?"

"No."

"He's been fired?"

"No."

"Then, what?"

"He's taking a leave of absence. Wait . . . he wants to tell you himself." She went to my door and called, "Warren . . . Warren . . . can you come in here?"

"I'm changing Tootsie," Dad called back. "Be there in just a minute."

"I thought Dad never changed a diaper in his life."

"He didn't. Not until Tootsie came along."

"What's so special about changing *her* diapers?" I asked.

"Nothing. It's just that Dad realizes he missed out on some of your baby experiences, and he doesn't want to make the same mistake again."

"He's so busy changing Tootsie, he hasn't got time for anybody else!"

"Peter, that's not fair," Mom said.

"What do you know about fair?"

Dad came into my room, smelling like baby lotion.

"I told Peter you have a surprise for him," Mom said.

"I'm taking the year off," Dad said. "And that way I'll have more time to spend with the family, because I'll be working at home. I'm going to write a book."

"A book?" I said.

"That's right. On the history of advertising and its effect on the American people."

"Couldn't you write something more interesting?" I asked. "Like a book about a kid who runs away because his parents decide to move without asking him first."

"Sounds like a good story," Dad said. "Maybe you should write it yourself."

"Maybe I will," I said. "And I'd like to know how we're going to eat, with you not working."

"We've got some money saved . . . and I'll probably get an advance for writing the book."

"Give it a chance, Peter," Mom said.

"I'll think about it," I told her. "But if I'm gone in the morning, don't be surprised."

And then, from the other room, we could hear Fudge singing himself to sleep. "*M-a-i-n-e* spells *Maine. F-u-d-g-e* spells *Fudgie. P-e-t-e-r* spells *Pee-tah. B-e-e-r* spells *whiskey*."

"Will you listen to that?" I said. "The kid should be a big hit in kindergarten."

4

Off the Wall

I told Jimmy Fargo about Princeton.

"You're moving?" he asked, like he couldn't believe it.

"Not exactly," I answered. "We're just going for a year."

"You're moving!" he said. "I can't believe it."

"Neither can I."

"You don't *have* to move," he said. "You could stay here if you really wanted to."

"You think I don't want to stay? I don't know anybody in Princeton. You think I want to go to some school where I don't have any friends?"

"Then tell your mother and father you refuse to go. That's what I'd do."

"But where would I live?"

"With me."

"But where would I sleep?"

"On the floor," Jimmy said. "It's good for your back to sleep on the floor."

I thought about sleeping on the floor for a year. And about living with Jimmy and his father. Mr. Fargo used to be an actor, but now he's a painter. He paints these weird-looking pictures of circles and triangles and squares. He's so absentminded that he only buys food when Jimmy reminds him. One time I looked in their refrigerator, and all they had was an empty bottle of wine, half an apple, and a salami and onion sandwich so old it had turned green.

"If you don't stay, I'm never going to talk to you again," Jimmy said. "I mean *never!*" He bent down and tied his shoelace. Jimmy's laces are always undone. "And I'm going to tell Sheila Tubman she can have your rock in the park," he added.

"You wouldn't!"

"Try me."

"Some friend you're turning out to be!"

"Same for you!" Jimmy turned and walked away, his hands stuffed deep into his pockets.

I thought of plenty more to say as soon as he was gone, but instead of running down the street after him, I went home.

"Is that you, Peter?" Mom called.

"No!" I went to my room and slammed my bedroom door. I was glad that I hadn't bothered to hang up my map of the world again. I took out my Kreskin's Crystal. Jimmy gave it to me on my last birthday. When I can't fall asleep at night, I hold the chain above the lucite base and watch the small ball swing from side to side. I concentrate on it until my eyes get this heavy feeling and want to close.

I opened my window enough to throw out my Kreskin's Crystal. I imagined it smashing into a zillion pieces on the sidewalk below. But suppose I had trouble falling asleep in Princeton. What would I do? I put it back in its box. There had to be a better way to get even with Jimmy Fargo.

Two hours later, I was still thinking up ways to get back at him, when the doorbell rang. And it was Jimmy.

"Changed my mind," he said. "And I'm sorry."

"Yeah . . . well . . . me too. . . ."

"I was disappointed, that's all. I don't want you to move . . . but there's nothing I can do about it. It's not your fault. . . ."

"That's what I was trying to tell you," I said.

"I know."

"Well . . ."

"My father says Princeton's just an hour by train."

"That's right."

"So I won't give Sheila your rock, after all."

"Thanks. She wouldn't know what to do with it anyway," I said.

"But I'm not going to use it until you come back."

"Okay. I won't use my Kreskin's Crystal until I get back, either."

"Deal!" Jimmy said.

And we shook on it.

o   o   o   o

The next morning when I was going down in the elevator with Turtle, Henry said, "I'm going to miss you and your family."

"Bet you won't miss Fudge," I said.

"Oh yes . . . even that little devil," Henry said. "I remember the day he got into my elevator and pushed all the buttons at once . . . jammed up the works for two hours." Henry laughed. He sounded like a sea lion. I always expect him to slap his arms together when he laughs. "And I'll miss that baby of yours, too. Won't get to see her grow up now."

"Sure you will," I told him. "We're only going for a year."

"That's what they all say," Henry muttered.

Outside, it was gray and humid. I wondered if the sun was shining in Princeton. As I walked Turtle down the street, he sniffed here and there, trying to find a place he liked. I encouraged him to use the curb. *In Princeton he'll be able to go wherever he likes*, I thought. Maybe I won't even have to walk him. I'll just open the door and he'll run out into the yard. And I won't have to clean up after him, either.

Ever since New York City passed what I call the Doggie-Do law, walking Turtle hasn't been that much fun. At first, when I heard that every dog owner had to clean up after his own dog, I told Mom that I wouldn't be able to walk Turtle anymore.

Mom said, "That's too bad, Peter. Because if you don't walk him, who will?"

I was hoping Mom would volunteer. I was hoping she'd say, "I know how grossed out you feel at the idea of picking up Turtle's dog-do. . . ."

But she didn't. Instead she said, "Look, Peter . . . you're going to have to make a tough decision. If you want to keep Turtle, you're going to have to clean up after him. Otherwise, Daddy and I will try to find a nice farm somewhere in the country and . . ."

I didn't wait for her to finish. "Send Turtle to a farm?" I shouted. "Are you kidding? He's a city dog! He's *my* dog!"

"Well, then . . ." Mom said, smiling.

I got the point.

Mom bought me a contraption called a Pooper-Scooper. It's a kind of shovel, attached to a Baggie, and when Turtle does his thing I scoop it up, get it into the Baggie, tie up the end, and toss it into the trash basket.

At first I made a mess of myself, trying to get it to

work. But now I'm a regular expert. Still, it's pretty disgusting. Almost as disgusting as Tootsie's diapers. I wish I could train Turtle to use the toilet, especially in winter, when I stand around freezing while he takes his time, trying to make up his mind. I know it's not Turtle's fault. He can't help being a dog. And when he sleeps at the foot of my bed or licks my face, it's all worth it.

Just as Turtle was finishing, Sheila Tubman came skipping up the street. "I hear you're moving," she said.

I nodded, and scooped up his stuff.

"Good! I was afraid it was just a rumor. I can't wait until you're gone. Then I won't have to smell your yucky dog anymore."

"My dog is not yucky!" I yelled, tying up the poop bag.

"Did you ever smell him, Peter?"

"Yes, all the time."

"Well, I guess you don't notice because you smell so much like him yourself." She started skipping away.

"Hey, Sheila . . ." I called.

"Yes?" She turned around.

"Stuff it!"

"Peter Hatcher, you are disgusting!"

"That's better than what you are," I called, enjoying myself.

"Oh yeah . . . what's that?" she asked.

"That's for me to know and you to find out."

"Ha ha, very funny," she said. "You and your yucky dog are both *very* funny!"

"*Sic her*, Turtle," I said. Turtle growled, then started barking, which *was* very funny, because he doesn't know what *sic her* means. But Sheila didn't know that *he* didn't know, so she started screaming and running toward our building. And when Turtle saw her go crazy like that, he took off after her, barking up a storm, thinking it was some kind of game. He pulled his leash right out of my hand, so I had to chase him, calling, "Turtle, Turtle . . . down boy," because he was already jumping up and down on Sheila, trying to lick her face.

Sheila kept right on screaming.

Finally Henry came out and asked, "What's going on here?" He pulled Turtle off Sheila and held him for me. I picked up the end of his leash and patted his head.

"It's Peter Hatcher," Sheila said. "He told his dumb dog to *sic* me and he did!"

"He did not!" I said.

"He did too!"

"You don't even know what *sic* means," I said.

"I certainly do!"

"Oh yeah . . . what?" I asked.

"It means . . . it's like . . . like giving germs to a

41

person," Sheila said. "The one he *sics* gets sick, too."

I started laughing. "Did you hear that, Henry? Did you hear what she said?"

"I heard," Henry said. "And I want you to keep your dog outside until he calms down." He turned to Sheila. "Come on, honey . . . I'll take you upstairs first."

"I'm so glad he's moving," Sheila sniffed. "I hope he never comes back. There should be a law . . ."

I laughed all the way to the corner. I think Turtle did too.

o   o   o   o

On the morning of the move, Mom woke me at six o'clock. I still had to pack my carton of special things. But first I wanted some juice. I'm always thirsty first thing in the morning. On my way to the kitchen I passed Tootsie's crib. She was watching her mobile and gurgling away. She was also covered with trading stamps. They were stuck to her arms, her legs, her belly, and her face. She even had one on the top of her head, and one pasted to the bottom of each foot. "Hey, Mom . . ." I called.

"What is it?"

"It's Tootsie."

"But I just . . ."

I didn't wait for her to finish. "Hurry up, Mom!" I called. Mom raced in, buttoning up her skirt. "Oh no!" she said when she saw Tootsie. Then she shouted, "Fudge!"

"Hello, Mommy," Fudge said, crawling out from under Tootsie's crib. He was wearing his disguise—black eyeglass frames attached to a rubber nose, with a stick-on beard and moustache. He'd sent away for it months ago. It cost four cereal box tops, plus twenty-five cents.

"Did you do that to Tootsie?"

"Yes, Mommy." He was using his best-little-boy-in-the-world voice.

"Why?" Mom asked.

"Tootsie told me to." He climbed up the side of her crib and reached in, shaking Tootsie a little. "Didn't you tell me to, good girl, good little baby. . . ."

Tootsie said, "Aaaa . . ." and she kicked her legs up in the air.

"That was a very naughty thing to do!" Mom told Fudge. "And I am very angry at you."

Fudge kissed my mother's hand. "I love you, Mommy."

"That's not going to work today," Mom told him.

"I love you anyway," he said, kissing her other hand. "You're the best mommy in the whole world. Don't you love your little boy?"

"Yes, I love you," she said, "but I am still very angry at you. VERY!" And she smacked Fudge on his backside.

He pouted for a minute, about to cry, then changed his mind. "Didn't hurt," he said.

"You want one that will hurt?" Mom asked.

"No!"

"Then don't you ever do anything like that again. Do you understand?"

"Yes!"

"Hey Mom," I said, "I thought you don't believe in violence."

"I don't, ordinarily," Mom said, "but sometimes I forget."

"Look . . . it's okay with me if you want to spank Fudge," I said. "Personally, I think a spanking a day would be good for him."

"No . . . no . . . no . . ." Fudge shouted, holding his rear end.

"Why'd you really do it?" I asked him.

"I want to trade her in for a two-wheeler, like yours," he told me.

"You can't trade her in," Mom said. "She's a person . . . she's not a book of stamps."

"She looks like a book of stamps," Fudge said.

Mom picked up Tootsie.

"Well, doesn't she?" Fudge asked again, and I could tell Mom was trying hard not to laugh.

"You know something, Fudge?" I said. "You're off the wall . . . you are *really* off the wall."

"Off the wall . . . off the wall . . ." he sang, dancing around Mom and Tootsie. "Fudgie is off the wall!"

Tootsie laughed. Either that or she hiccuped. It's hard to tell the difference.

I followed Mom into the bathroom, where she set Tootsie in the sink.

"Two years of trading stamps, down the drain," I said.

"Good-bye stamps," Fudge called from the doorway. "Good-bye . . . good-bye . . ."

"I'm not going to save stamps anymore," Mom said. "I'm going to find a grocery store that gives away something else."

o o o o

An hour later Dad came back with the U-Haul, and we loaded it and were on our way.

As soon as we were through the Lincoln Tunnel, Fudge started singing, "*M-a-i-n-e* spells *Princeton*."

"No, it doesn't stupid," I said. "It spells *Maine*."

"I know," Fudge said. "I'm just making up a song."

"Maybe you could make it up in your head," Dad suggested. "And sing it to us when we get to Princeton. Then it will be a surprise."

"A surprise," Fudge said. "I like surprises." He was quiet for a minute. Then he said, "You know what, Daddy? I'm off the wall."

"Who told you that?" Dad asked.

"Pee-tah. Didn't you?" he asked me.

"Yeah," I said. "I sure did. And you sure are."

"I'm off the wall," Fudge repeated. "Just like Pee-tah's map of the world." He rested his head against Mom's shoulder and I could hear him slurping away on his fingers. He was still wearing his disguise.

5

Small Ones Are Sweeter.

Our house, that is, Millie and George's house, is so old that the bathtub stands off the floor, on legs. And the hot and cold water don't come out of the same faucet, so when you're washing your hands, you either freeze them or burn them. Mom says you're supposed to put the plug in the sink and mix the water in the basin. But that's a lot of trouble. At least we don't have chamber pots. The toilets actually flush.

Outside, the house is painted yellow and the shutters are white. The windows and doorways are slightly crooked. Dad says that's part of the charm of the house. I know better than to tell him what I think. Inside, the floors are wooden and they creak when you walk across them.

Downstairs, there is a living room with a piano, a dining room with a table so big you have to shout to make yourself heard, a kitchen with pots and pans hanging all over the place, and a library, where the walls are lined with books, arranged according to color. There's a brown leather section, a green leather section, a red leather section and a tan leather section. Upstairs, there are four bedrooms, all in a row. And everywhere you look there are fireplaces. There's one in every bedroom, there's one in the living room, another in the dining room and still another in the library. There aren't any in the bathrooms or the kitchen.

My mother and father call the house *fantastic*, *fabulous*, *unbelievable*. I hear them talking to their friends on the phone, and those are the dumb words they use to describe this place.

Our neighborhood is a lot like our house. Old. Every house on the block is a lot like this one, with a small front yard and a big backyard. In our backyard we have George's rose garden and Millie's herb and vegetable garden. The first day we were here, Dad bought a stack of books with titles like *Know Your Roses*, *Know Your Herbs*, *Organic Vegetables and You*, and my favorite, *The Agony of Beetles in Your Garden*.

"You didn't have to worry about beetles in New York, did you, Dad?" I said at dinner.

"That's enough, Peter," Dad said to me.

"That's enough, Pee-tah," Fudge repeated.

"Cut that out!" I told him.

"Cut that out!" he said back to me.

Fudge's new game is repeating everything I say. He's really driving me crazy this time.

"Pass the salt, please," I said to Mom.

"Pass the salt, please," he said, laughing.

I pushed back my chair. "I can't take it anymore. I mean it. Do something, will you?" I begged my parents.

But he was already at it. "I can't take it anymore. Do something, will you . . ." And he laughed so hard he choked.

Dad turned him upside down and whacked him on the back.

"I want you to stop doing that, Fudge," he said. "Do you understand?"

I don't know why my parents are always asking him if he understands. He understands just fine. That has nothing to do with it.

Fudge nodded.

"Because if you don't stop repeating everything that Peter says, I'm going to do more than just whack your back. Get it?"

I couldn't help smiling.

o   o   o   o

Mom has this thing that's called a Snugli for carrying Tootsie. She hangs it around her neck and Tootsie fits into it and rides right next to Mom's middle. It looks very comfortable. Sometimes Dad carries Tootsie in it, too. Mom says they didn't have them when I was a baby. I missed out on a lot of good things.

Every night after supper, we walk into town, stopping at Baskin-Robbins for ice cream. One night Mom asked me if I would like to wear the sling and carry Tootsie.

"No, thanks!" I said. "I wouldn't be caught dead wearing a baby around my neck."

"Oh, Peter, you're so silly."

Baskin-Robbins is having a contest. They're looking for names for a new ice-cream flavor. So far I've suggested Lemon Lunatic, Crazy Chocolate, and Miserable Mint.

o   o   o   o

After almost two weeks of hanging around the house, I actually met a kid my age. He lives across the street, but he was at scout camp when we first moved here. His name is Alex Santo and he's going into sixth grade too. He's very small, with hair that hangs into his eyes, and he's always wearing a T-shirt that says Princeton, Class of '91. By the time I met him, I was so lonely and bored I wouldn't have cared if he had three heads, as long as he was my age and wanted to be friends.

Alex came over one morning and said, "You want to go into business with me?"

"What kind of business?" I asked.

"Worms," he told me.

"Worms?" I asked.

"Yeah, worms," he said again.

"Worms!" Fudge said, jumping down the front steps. "Wormy wormy worms!"

Alex looked over at him.

"Don't mind him," I said. "He's just my little brother."

"Oh," Alex said. "So what do you say?"

"Sure," I told him, having no idea what kind of worm business Alex was talking about. "When do I start?"

"How about now?" Alex asked.

"Okay. What do I do?"

"First we dig them up. Then we sell them to Mrs. Muldour, down the street. She pays five cents a worm."

"What does she do with them?" I asked.

"She doesn't say. Some people think she uses them for fishing. Other people think she uses them in her garden. Personally . . ." He stopped and scratched his head.

"Go on . . . go on. . . ."

"I think she eats them," Alex said.

I thought for a minute. "Worm pie?"

"Yeah . . . and worm stew . . . and worm juice. . . ."

"And worm soup," I said, getting warmed up. "And worm bread."

"Oh yeah, that's the best," Alex said. "Nice soft bread with little worms here and there. . . ."

"You can make a really tasty worm and cheese sandwich on it," I said. We were doubled over now, laughing our heads off.

"And worm ice cream," Fudge said, jumping on top of us.

"Worm ice cream," Alex and I said together.

I decided that with Alex Santo in my class, Princeton might not be too bad.

That afternoon Alex and I went digging for worms. We rode our bikes over to the lake. It's easy to ride in Princeton, because they have bike paths on every street. Alex had a pail and a couple of shovels, and we got to work. Finding worms was no problem. An hour later we rode back to my house.

"Mrs. Muldour likes her worms clean," Alex told me, turning on our hose.

"That figures, if she uses them for cooking," I said.

We left the pail of worms outside and went in for a drink. When we came out, Fudge was standing next to Tootsie's carriage, dangling a worm in front of her.

"Cut that out!" I yelled, racing over to him.

"Why? She likes it," Fudge said. "Watch. . . ."

Alex and I looked into Tootsie's carriage. She laughed every time Fudge held up the worm.

"You're right," I said. "She does like it. Hey, Mom . . . look at this. . . ."

"What is it?" Mom called from where she was weeding Millie's organically grown vegetables.

"You've got to see for yourself," I called back.

She came over, wiping her hands on her jeans.

"Watch, Mommy," Fudge said, and he took the worm from behind his back and dangled it over Tootsie's carriage.

She smiled and gurgled.

But Mom screamed. "Get that thing out of here. Hurry up . . . get rid of it . . . now."

"It's just a worm, Mommy. Don't you like worms?"

"No, I don't. I really don't like worms at all. And I never want you to show me another one. Do you understand?"

Fudge put the worm on his arm and let it crawl up to his shoulder. "See . . . isn't he cute? I'm going to call him Willy. Willy Worm. And he'll be my very own pet. I'm going to sleep with him, and he can eat next to me at the table, and he'll take a bath with me. . . ."

"Fudge!"

"Yes, Mommy?"

"I told you, I don't ever want to see that worm again. And you may *not* bring him into the house. And you may *not* hold him that close to Tootsie. Do you understand me this time?"

"You really don't like worms?" Fudge said.

"That's right," Mom said. "I really don't."

"Why not?" Fudge asked.

"It's nothing I can explain." Mom went back to weeding the garden. Fudge followed her.

"Is your family always like that?" Alex asked.

"You haven't seen anything yet!" I told him.

o o o o

On our way to Mrs. Muldour's house, I thought I remembered reading that worms regenerate when you cut them in half. But I wasn't sure. So I asked Alex if he'd ever tried that.

"Sure," Alex said, "plenty of times."

"And what happens?"

"Nothing. You get two little worms."

"Right. And if Mrs. Muldour pays you five cents a worm . . ."

A slow smile spread across Alex's face. "I see what you mean," he said. "How come I never thought of that?"

I didn't answer.

We dumped our worms out on the sidewalk and cut all but one in half. That one was big enough to cut into thirds. So now, instead of sixteen worms, we had thirty-three.

Mrs. Muldour lived in an old house that was painted gray, with blue shutters. Alex rang her bell. A big, round woman with hair the color of her house and glasses halfway down her nose came to the door.

She wore sneakers and blue jeans and a red and white shirt.

"Well, hello Alex . . . long time no see."

"Hi, Mrs. Muldour," Alex said. "I've got a partner now."

She looked at me over the rims of her glasses.

"I'm Peter Hatcher. We just moved in down the street." She kept looking at me, so I kept talking. "In the Wentmans' house . . . Millie and George Wentman . . . they're friends of my mother and father . . . we're just here for the year . . . to see how we like being away from the city. . . ."

"Are you finished?" she asked.

"Yes."

"Good. Then let's get down to business."

"We've got thirty-three for you today, Mrs. Muldour," Alex said. "Real beauties."

"Thirty-three . . ." She held up the jar and studied them. "They look awfully small."

"Small ones are sweeter," I said.

She gave me a strange look this time.

So I quickly added, "They'll get bigger later in the summer."

"Really? I should think they'd be at their best now."

"Oh no," I told her. "They'll be getting fatter and longer by August, and by September they'll be in their prime."

"Is that a fact?" she asked.

"Uh huh," I said, praying that she wouldn't guess I didn't know what I was talking about.

"Well, live and learn," Mrs. Muldour said. She went inside and came back with her wallet. "You know," she told us, "I could go down to the filling station and buy a container of worms, but I think freshly dug ones are so much better." She opened her wallet. "Let's see . . . five cents times thirty-three worms . . . that's one dollar and fifty cents." She handed the money to Alex.

"Excuse me, Mrs. Muldour," Alex said, "but it's one, sixty-five."

Mrs. Muldour laughed. "Can't fool you, can I, Alex?"

"No, Mrs. Muldour, not when it comes to math. Would you like more worms next week?"

"Of course. As many as you can bring me. You can't have too many worms, you know."

Alex gave me a look, and we thanked Mrs. Muldour and walked away. Once we were out of earshot, Alex said, "Small ones are sweeter . . ." and he gave me an elbow in the ribs.

"Worm soup tonight," I told him. And we exploded, laughing.

o　o　o　o

After supper, Mom got Tootsie into her sling, and the five of us went off to Baskin-Robbins. When we got there, Fudge walked up to the girl behind the counter and said, "Worm ice cream."

"Beg pardon?" the girl said.

"Worm ice cream," he repeated.

"We don't have . . ."

"For flavor of the month," Fudge told her. "Worm ice cream."

"Are you saying . . ." she began.

"Yes, he is," I said. "Worm . . . that's *w-o-r-m*."

"I can spell," the girl said, annoyed. "But I really don't think that people would go for that flavor."

"Some people would. Right, Pee-tah?"

"Sure," I said. "Some people right in this town might think it's terrific."

"Look, kids . . . we're very busy tonight, so cut out the wise-guy stuff and tell me what you want."

"I'll have a chocolate-chip–mint sundae with the works," I told her.

"And I'll have a fudge ripple cone," Fudge said. "Just like my name."

"Oh, your name is Cone?" she asked.

"No."

"Ripple?"

"No."

"I suppose you're going to tell me it's Fudge . . . right?"

"That's right," Fudge said, chinning himself on the counter.

"Cute kid," she mumbled to herself. "Real cute."

6

Farley Drexel
Meets Rat Face.

In August, Turtle needed his yearly checkup and shots. Mom and Dad asked around and decided on The Ark, an animal hospital near the highway. To get there we drove through town, on a bridge over the lake where Alex and I dug worms, up a long hill, and all the way out to the traffic circle. It seemed to me they could have found some place closer.

Turtle always shakes when he goes to the vet's. I don't know how he knows he's going to get his shots, but he does. I tried talking to him softly, telling him it would only hurt for a second, but he whined and cowered in the corner anyway.

On the way back, we stopped off at Sandy's Bakery near the traffic circle. They make the best brownies I've ever tasted, and without nuts. Mom is allergic to nuts, which means she can't even eat peanut butter. Without peanut butter, I might starve.

o   o   o   o

The week before school started, I had a lot of trouble falling asleep. It was too quiet in Princeton. I missed the sounds of the city. I tried not to think of my Kreskin's Crystal, sitting in its box, on the shelf in my closet. I tried counting sheep and reciting the alphabet backwards, instead. But when that didn't work, I just couldn't help myself. I jumped out of bed and got it. As I held it up, I imagined Kreskin himself standing at the foot of my bed chanting, "Sleep . . . sleep. . . ."

I woke up the next morning with my Kreskin's Crystal under me. I had a pain in my butt from sleeping on top of it. And I felt really guilty about having used it at all. I'd cheated on Jimmy Fargo. We'd made a deal, and I'd broken it. Some friend I was! I wanted to tell him that it was okay with me if he decided to use our rock. But Jimmy was in Vermont, with his mother, and they had no phone up there.

And I wasn't the only one who was having trouble sleeping.

"I can't sleep anymore," Fudge said, at breakfast.

"Why not?" Dad asked.

"I'm afraid."

"Of what?" Dad said.

"Monsters!"

"There are no monsters," Dad told him.

"How do you know?"

"Because I do," Dad said, spreading strawberry jam on his toast.

"Did you learn it at college?" Fudge asked, making mush out of his cereal.

"No."

"Then where did you learn it?" Fudge asked.

Dad sipped his coffee. Then he said, "I uh . . . learned it in high school."

"Come on, Dad," I said, laughing.

Dad gave me a look that let me know I should keep quiet. I wondered if he and Mom had told me ridiculous things like that when I was a little kid. And if I'd believed them.

"I'm still afraid," Fudge said. "I want to sleep in Pee-tah's room."

"No way," I said. "There is no way I'm going to have him in my room. He talks in his sleep."

"Then I'll sleep with Mommy," Fudge announced.

My mother, who had been reading the morning paper, looked up. "What?" she asked.

"From now on I'm sleeping with you," Fudge said.

"You have your own room, Fudgie," Mom told him, "with your own big-boy bed."

"I don't want my own room!" he shouted. "I want to share. Sharing is better. You always say so!"

Mom sighed. "That's different," she said. "Sharing is for toys and cookies and . . ."

"Maybe if Turtle sleeps with Fudge . . ." Dad began.

But I didn't wait for him to finish. "Hey, wait a minute . . . Turtle is *my* dog . . . remember?"

"But you're willing to share him, aren't you, Peter?" Dad asked.

"Not at night. He sleeps with me!"

Fudge started to cry. "Nobody cares about Fudgie. Nobody cares if the monsters eat him up!"

"Nobody's going to eat you up," Mom said.

"How do you know?" Fudge asked.

"Because I do, that's how," Mom said.

"Did you learn it in high school?"

"Uh . . . excuse me," I said, getting up from the table. "But this is where I came in."

Fudge solved his problem by himself. Every night, after the rest of the family had gone to sleep, Fudge dragged his Snoopy sleeping bag down the hall and parked himself in front of Mom and Dad's bedroom, where he slept.

And Mom and Dad didn't do a thing about it. They'd just get up in the morning and step right over him. They told each other it was just another phase. That he'd get over it. If Fudge wasn't going through one phase, he was going through another. I couldn't help thinking that one of these days Tootsie would be going through phases too. The way it looked now, there might be no end.

○　○　○　○

On the day before school started, Alex and I rode our bikes to the shopping center to buy our school supplies. That reminded me of Jimmy Fargo and how we always used to go shopping for school supplies together. I felt really lonely, thinking about Jimmy, and scared about what school would be like here. Maybe all the kids would hate me. Maybe I'd hate them. Maybe we'd hate each other. Maybe I'd get a dumb teacher. Dumb teachers are the worst. I should know. I had one in third grade.

That night I didn't even try to get to sleep without my Kreskin's Crystal. Even so, I woke up about a million times during the night.

The next morning, I asked Mom how she expected me to walk Fudge to school and still ride my bike with Alex. Because Alex told me that all the kids in Princeton ride bikes to school.

"Maybe you could ride slowly and Fudge could walk beside you," she said.

"Come on, Mom!"

"Well, maybe you could walk him until he knows the way by himself."

"That might take all year," I said. "Besides, I want to go to school with Alex."

"Look, Peter . . . how about if you just walk him the first week and then we'll see what happens?"

"I don't think you understand, Mom . . . sixth graders don't walk kindergarten babies to school at all."

"And I don't think *you* understand how disappointed Fudgie's going to be," Mom said, slamming the refrigerator door. "But if that's the way you feel about it, I'll take him myself!"

"Good idea," I told her.

But Fudge, who'd been listening behind the kitchen door, shouted, "No! I want to go to school with Pee-tah. You promised," he told Mom. "You promised!"

Mom looked at me, as if to say "You see?"

"Oh, all right," I said. "I'll ride and you can follow me."

"I'll ride, too."

"You don't have a bike."

"I have a Toddle-Bike."

"You can't ride a Toddle-Bike to school."

"Why not?"

"Because you can't. Now, hurry up. I don't want to be late on the first day."

Alex was waiting for me outside. We headed for school. Fudge tried hard to keep up with us, running alongside our bikes, panting all the way. We were going really slow, but still, he couldn't make it. I felt sorry for the kid. It wasn't his fault he was just a kindergarten baby. So I scooped him up and sat him on the crossbar of my bicycle, even though my parents have warned me a million times never to do that. I think they once knew someone who smashed his head open that way. But what they didn't know wouldn't hurt them. Besides, the school wasn't that far. And Fudge really liked riding on my bar. He waved to everybody on the street. "I'm starting kindergarten today," he sang.

Alex, who had no brothers or sisters, laughed.

When we got to school, I took Fudge to Mrs. Hildebrandt's kindergarten and handed her Fudge's registration card. Then I went upstairs with Alex to Mr. Bogner's sixth grade. All the kids were singing,

> Oh who owns the school?
> Oh who owns the school?
> Oh who owns the school?
>   the people saaaayyyy. . . .
>
> Oh we own the school
> Oh we own the school
> 'Cause we are sixth
>   graaaaders today!

I sat down at a desk next to Alex. On my other side was a girl, about three heads taller than me, with long, tangled brown hair.

Mr. Bogner wasn't dumb. I could tell right off. I can always tell. First he told us about his summer.

He was an Outward Bound instructor in Colorado. He taught college kids to climb mountains. Then we told him what we did over the summer. I would have liked mine to sound more exciting. I would have liked to tell the class—*"This summer I sailed the Atlantic with just my dog, Turtle, and my friend, Jimmy Fargo. Oh sure, we had some rough times but we made it across."* Except that Alex was sitting right there and he knew the truth.

There were three new kids in our class. I was the only one from New York. Another boy, Harvey, was from Pennsylvania, and a girl, Martha, was from Minnesota.

Mr. Bogner told us about some of the projects we'd be working on during the year, like building a Viking ship and studying our home state of New Jersey. I wanted to tell him that it wasn't my home state and it never would be, but before I had a chance, Martha said, "Excuse me, Mr. Bogner, but my home state is Minnesota. So will I be studying that, while the rest of the class does New Jersey?"

"No, Martha," Mr. Bogner said. "As long as you're living here, you can consider New Jersey your home state."

"But Mr. Bogner . . ." Martha said.

"Why don't you see me about it after class?" Mr. Bogner said. And he didn't sound angry or anything.

Later, I found out the girl who was sitting next to me, the tall one with the tangled hair, is named

Joanne McFadden. I was going to ask her where she lived, when a message came over the intercom. "Good morning, Mr. Bogner . . . would you send Peter Hatcher to Mr. Green's office, please?"

"Right away," Mr. Bogner answered.

"Thank yooooou."

Mr. Green was the principal. What did he want with me?

Joanne McFadden whispered, "What'd you do?"

"I don't know," I said, feeling my face turn red.

"Do you know where Mr. Green's office is?" Mr. Bogner asked.

"I'll find it," I said.

"Don't look so worried, Peter," Mr. Bogner said. "You can't be in that much trouble . . . it's only the first day of school."

The whole class laughed, except Joanne McFadden. She just gave me a kind of shy smile.

It probably has something to do with registration, I thought, on my way to the office. *I'll bet my mother didn't fill out the part of the registration card, about who to call in case of emergency if the parents can't be reached. She forgets that almost every year. Or maybe the principal likes to introduce himself personally to all the new students. But then, why wouldn't he have asked for Harvey too? And Martha, from Minnesota? Because he calls them to his office in alphabetical order*, I told myself, not knowing either Harvey's or Martha's last names. *And if he started with the* A's *early this morning, he'd probably be up to the* H's *now. Yes, that made sense.*

I found Mr. Green's office. "I'm Peter Hatcher," I told his secretary.

"Go right in," she said. "He's expecting you."

"You wanted to meet me?" I said to Mr. Green. "I mean . . . see me?"

"Hello, Peter." Mr. Green looked something like my uncle, but my uncle is clean-shaven and Mr. Green had a moustache. Now that my father is growing a beard, I'm more aware of these things. "We're having a bit of a problem with your brother," Mr. Green said.

Oh, so that was it. I should have known!

"We've tried to get your mother or father on the phone, but there's no answer, so we were hoping you'd be willing to help us."

"What'd he do this time?" I asked.

"A number of things," Mr. Green said. "Come on down to the kindergarten . . . I'll show you."

We walked down the hall together.

o o o o

All the kindergarten babies were busy. Some were building with blocks, others were painting, and a group was playing house in the corner. It was just the way I remembered kindergarten. But I didn't see Fudge anywhere.

"Oh, Mr. Green," Mrs. Hildebrandt said, limping

over to us. "I'm so glad you're here. I can't do a thing with him. He still refuses to come down."

I looked up. Fudge was perched on top of the cabinets that were on top of the cubbies. He was stretched out, lying across the top, just inches from the ceiling.

"Hi, Pee-tah," he called, waving.

"What are you doing up there?" I said.

"Resting."

"Come on down!"

"No. I don't like this school. I quit!"

"You can't quit," Mr. Green said.

"Why not?" Fudge asked.

"Because going to school is your job," Mr. Green said. "Otherwise, what will you be when you grow up?"

"A bird!" Fudge told him.

Mr. Green laughed. "Creative, isn't he?"

"I wouldn't necessarily call it that," Mrs. Hildebrandt said.

"Why'd he climb up there in the first place?" I asked.

"Well," Mrs. Hildebrandt said, "*that* is a long story."

"Because she's mean!" Fudge called. "*M-e-a-n.*"

"Now, Mr. Green," Mrs. Hildebrandt said, "you've known me for a long time . . . and I ask you . . . have I ever been mean to a child . . . knowingly, consciously, intentionally mean? Especially on the first day of school?"

"She wouldn't call me *Fudge*," Fudge said. "That's why I had to kick her!"

"He kicked you?" I asked Mrs. Hildebrandt.

She held up her skirt and showed me her bruised shin. "And I don't mind telling you," she said, "that I was in great pain. I almost passed out . . . right in front of the children."

"Is that when he climbed to the top of the cabinets?" I asked.

"That is correct."

"Because she wouldn't call me *Fudge*," Fudge said again.

"It's not a proper name," Mrs. Hildebrandt said. "And it's not as if he hasn't got a proper name. He has. *Farley Drexel Hatcher*. I told him that I would call him Farley . . . or I would call him Drexel . . . or I would call him F. D."

"But she wouldn't call me *Fudge!*"

All the little kids turned around, and suddenly the room was very quiet.

"That's right," Mrs. Hildebrandt said. "Fudge is a good name for candy. It is not a good name for a boy."

"I told you, I'm a bird," Fudge shouted.

"There is something very definitely wrong with that child," Mrs. Hildebrandt said.

"There's nothing wrong with him!" I said. "My mother calls him Fudge. My father calls him Fudge. My grandmother calls him Fudge. His friends call him Fudge. My friends call him Fudge. I call him Fudge. He calls himself Fudge. . . ."

"Yes, we get the picture," Mr. Green said.

"I can't imagine a parent actually deciding to call a child Fudge," Mrs. Hildebrandt said.

"You don't know my parents," I told her.

"Well, that's true, but . . ."

"I think what we have here is a basic personality conflict," Mr. Green said. "So I suggest that we transfer Fudge to Ms. Ziff's kindergarten."

"Splendid idea!" Mrs. Hildebrandt said. "The sooner, the better."

"You can come down now," I told Fudge. "You're going into the other kindergarten."

"Will the teacher call me Fudge?" he asked.

"As long as you want her to," Mr. Green said.

"And will she let me use the round blocks?"

Mr. Green looked at Mrs. Hildebrandt.

"I never let them use the round blocks on the first day. It's one of my rules."

"You can't build anything good without the round blocks," Fudge said.

"We'll ask Ms. Ziff," Mr. Green told Fudge. "But we do have rules here . . . and you will have to obey them."

"As long as I can use the round blocks," Fudge said.

Mr. Green loosened his shirt collar and wiped off his forehead with a handkerchief.

"Hurry up," I said to Fudge. "I'm missing important things upstairs."

"Like what?"

"Never mind . . . just get down."

Fudge climbed down to the top of the cubbies, and Mr. Green reached up and lifted him the rest of the way down.

"Good-bye, Farley Drexel," Mrs. Hildebrandt said.

"Good-bye, Rat Face," Fudge said to her.

I gave him an elbow and whispered, "You don't go around calling teachers Rat Face."

"Not even if they have one?" he asked.

"Not even then," I said.

Mr. Green and I took Fudge next door, to Ms. Ziff's kindergarten. She was reading *Arthur the Anteater* to the kids. I could tell that Fudge was impressed. "I know that story," he said. "Arthur doesn't like to eat red ants."

Mr. Green handed Ms. Ziff Fudge's registration card. "His name is Farley Drexel," Mr. Green said. "But everybody calls him Fudge."

Ms. Ziff smiled at Fudge. "And I'll bet you're as sweet as your name," she said.

"I am," Fudge agreed.

"Just ask Mrs. Hildebrandt," I said to myself. My brother's school career had begun.

7

A Very Cultured Bird

Every day Fudge brought home paintings from his kindergarten class. Mom hung them on the wall in the kitchen. One night she said, "Fudgie, you're doing so well in school, I'm going to get you a special treat. What would you like?"

"A bird," Fudge said, as if he'd been thinking about it for years.

"A bird?" Mom repeated.

"Yes. My very own bird."

"A bird," Dad said, scratching his new beard.

"I was thinking more in terms of a yo-yo," Mom said.

"I have a yo-yo," Fudge told her. "But I don't have a bird."

"I don't see why we can't get Fudge a bird," Dad said. "It might be nice for him to have his own pet."

"But, Warren," Mom said. "Do you really think he's ready for his own pet?"

"Yes," Dad said. "I do."

"Well . . ." Mom said, and I could see her thinking it over, "if it's all right with Daddy, then it's all right with me."

"And he can sleep in my room, right?" Fudge asked.

"Yes," Dad said.

"On my bed?"

"No," Dad said. "Birds sleep in cages, not beds."

"But I would be very careful," Fudge said. "I would keep him under the covers with me."

"Birds can't sleep in beds," Mom said.

"Why not?" Fudge asked.

"Because they like to sleep standing up," Mom said.

"They do?" Fudge asked.

"Yes."

"I think I'll try that tonight," Fudge said.

"People lie down to go to sleep," Dad explained. "Birds stand up. That's just one difference between people and birds."

"Another is that birds can fly . . . right?" Fudge asked.

"That's right," Dad said.

"Someday I might be able to fly . . . just like a bird!"

"Don't count on it," I said.

But he wasn't listening. He was dancing around Tootsie's high chair singing, "My very own bird, bird, bird . . ."

"Da ba," Tootsie said, tossing her rattle to the floor. That's her latest game. She throws down her toys, then screams until one of us picks them up for her. As soon as she has them back, she throws them down again. Some game!

Also, she's teething, so her gums are sore, so she screams a lot. She has this plastic teething ring that we keep in the freezer for her. She likes to bite on it. The cold numbs her gums.

The truth is, she'll bite on anything she can get into her mouth, including her toes. I keep telling my mother that it's not a good idea to let Tootsie grow up with her feet in her mouth. But Mom says it's just a phase and that she'll get over it. She even took out the family photo album to show me a picture of myself when I was about Tootsie's age. I had my toes in my mouth, too.

I've asked Mom to get rid of that picture, along with the one of me naked, holding a broom. If *that* one ever got out, I'd never hear the end of it.

Fudge asked Mom if he could bring Tootsie to school for Show and Tell. He wanted to repeat his lecture on *How Babies Are Made* for his kindergarten class. Mom phoned Ms. Ziff, who thought it was a wonderful idea, but before they went ahead with it, Ms. Ziff had to check it out with Mr. Green. Mr. Green said *absolutely not*, so that was the end of that. Fudge was disappointed, but Mom and Dad convinced him that once he got his bird, he'd have something even more exciting for Show and Tell.

◇ ◇ ◇ ◇

Grandma came to visit for a few days.

"I'm getting a bird," Fudge told her.

"What kind of bird are you going to get?" Grandma asked.

"I don't know. What kind of bird am I going to get?" he asked the rest of us.

We all spoke at once.

"A canary," Mom said.

"A parakeet," Dad said.

"A myna bird," I said.

Fudge looked confused.

Grandma said, "I see you haven't decided yet."

"Myna birds can talk," I said.

"A talking bird?" Fudge asked.

"Yes. You can teach a myna bird to say anything," I added.

"Anything?" Fudge asked, and I could tell what he was thinking.

"Well, almost anything," I told him.

"A talking bird," Fudge said, smiling. "Fudgie's going to get a talking bird."

"Now, wait a minute," Dad said. "We haven't decided on what kind of bird we're getting. I was thinking in terms of a nice blue parakeet. You can train a parakeet to fly around the room and land on a stick."

"And I was thinking in terms of a pretty yellow canary," Mom said. "Canaries can sing. They make everyone feel happy."

"That's nice," Fudge said. "Mommy can get a canary and Daddy can get a parakeet and Fudgie can get his myna bird."

"We're only getting one bird," Mom told him.

"Oh," Fudge said. "Then I guess Mommy won't get her canary and Daddy won't get his parakeet, because Fudgie's getting his myna bird. Pee-tah says they can talk and he knows everything."

Mom and Dad looked at me.

"Well, how was I supposed to know you wanted a canary?" I asked Mom. "And that you wanted a parakeet?" I asked Dad. "You never mentioned it before."

"It should be very educational for Fudgie to have a myna bird," Grandma said.

"If I teach him to talk, he might teach me to fly," Fudge said, flapping his arms.

Tootsie hiccuped, then started crying.

"Who wants some home-baked cookies?" Grandma

asked as she lifted Tootsie out of her high chair and patted her on the back.

Grandma is very good at changing the subject.

o o o o

The next afternoon when I got home from school, the car was gone and the house was quiet. I went upstairs and was on my way to my room when I heard something funny coming from Tootsie's room. Her door was opened just a crack and I peeked in. There was Grandma, barefooted, dancing in circles, with Tootsie in her arms. She was singing:

> Toot, Toot, Tootsie, good-bye!
> Toot, Toot, Tootsie, don't cry,
> The choo choo train that takes me,
> La da da dee dum doo dah dee dah
>   oh bah shoo dah,
> Kiss me, Tootsie, and then . . .

"Hi, Grandma," I said, opening the door all the way.

"Oh, Peter!" She stopped and her face turned red.

"What were you doing?" I asked.

"Dancing," she said. "Tootsie likes to dance, you know."

"No, I didn't know."

Tootsie grabbed a handful of Grandma's hair and screeched with delight.

"What was that song you were singing?" I asked.

" 'Toot, Toot, Tootsie! Good-bye'," Grandma said.

"You mean there really is such a song? You weren't making it up?"

"Certainly not! It was very popular back in . . . let's see . . . oh, I can't remember the year . . . but it was very popular."

Tootsie bounced up and down in Grandma's arms, wanting more. Grandma passed her to me. "Here, you try it now."

"Me?" I said. "You want *me* to dance with Tootsie?"

"Why not?"

"Grandma! I'm in sixth grade. I don't go around dancing with babies in my arms."

"Why not?"

"Well, because . . ."

"Come on," Grandma said. "I'll sing . . . you dance." And she began her song again.

Toot, Toot, Tootsie, good-bye!
Toot, Toot, Tootsie, don't cry. . . .

I twirled around and around with Tootsie in my arms, and Grandma was right, she loved it. She screamed and laughed and threw her head back, and pretty soon I was laughing too, and all three of us were having a fine old time when Fudge appeared at the door and said, "What are you doing, Pee-tah?"

I looked over, and Mom and Dad were standing there too.

"Oh, I uh . . . that is . . . I was . . ."

"Dancing," Grandma said. "Tootsie likes to dance, so we were dancing with her." She found her shoes under Tootsie's crib and stepped into them.

I put Tootsie down in her infant seat and smoothed my hair with my hands, ready to explain that it was Grandma's idea, that I was just going along with her. But it turned out that I didn't need to explain anything. Because nobody seemed to think it was strange that I was dancing with Tootsie or that Grandma was singing her "Toot, Toot, Tootsie! Good-bye" song.

"Guess what?" Fudge said.

"What?" Grandma asked.

"I saw him. . . . I saw my myna bird!"

"Where?" I asked.

"At the pet store," Fudge said. "We're going to bring him home tomorrow. They had to order a cage. He's all black, with yellow legs and a yellow nose."

"Yellow bill," I said.

"Nose, bill . . . who cares?" Fudge said. "And he can talk!"

"What can he say?"

"He can say *hello*, in French."

"In French?" I asked.

"That's right, in French," Mom said. "He's very cultured."

"And I've already named him." Fudge said.

"What did you name him?" Grandma asked.

I expected him to say Pierre or Jacques, since he speaks French.

"Uncle Feather," Fudge said.

"Uncle Feather?" I said.

"Yes, Uncle Feather," Fudge said again. "Isn't that a good name for a bird?"

"It's uh . . . unusual," I said.

"And interesting, right?" Fudge asked.

"Oh, yes . . . definitely interesting," I told him.

"It's a real privilege," Fudge said, "isn't it?"

"No, it's not a privilege," I told him. "It has nothing to do with privilege." I never should have used that word with such a little kid. He still didn't know how to use it. He probably never would.

"So it's not a privilege," Fudge said. "So who cares?" And he began to sing:

> Uncle Feather came to town,
> Flying in the blue sky,
> Yellow nose and yellow legs
> And he belongs to me oh my . . .

"Come on, Grandma," Fudge said, "dance with *me*, now." He and Grandma held hands and danced around the room while Fudge sang his latest, to the tune of "Yankee Doodle."

My family and their musical numbers were getting to be too much, so I took off for Alex's house and some peace and quiet.

o   o   o   o

The next day, Mom, Dad and Fudge went down to the pet store and returned with Uncle Feather, complete with cage, cover, a box of food and a book called *Getting To Know Your Myna Bird*.

"Bonjour . . . bonjour . . ." Uncle Feather said, over and over again.

"That means *hello* in French," Fudge told me, as if I didn't already know.

Dad carried the cage up to Fudge's room, which happened to be next to my room, and all afternoon all I heard was bonjour . . . bonjour, in bird-voice. I banged on the wall between my room and Fudge's. "Can't you teach him to say something else?"

"I'm trying . . . I'm trying . . ." Fudge hollered.

"I'm trying . . . I'm trying . . ." Uncle Feather repeated.

Swell, I thought. *We just got Fudge out of the habit of repeating everything I said, and now we've got a bird who does the same thing. Why didn't I keep my big mouth shut at the dinner table that night? Why didn't I convince Fudge to listen to Mom and get a canary, or to Dad, and get a parakeet?*

The next morning, when I went to have a look at Uncle Feather, he greeted me with, "Bonjour, stupid. . . ."

"Isn't he smart?" Fudge asked. "Doesn't he learn fast?"

"Yeah . . . he's terrific!" I said.

As I left the room, Uncle Feather called out, "Good-bye, stupid . . . good-bye. . . ."

"Good-bye, yourself," I said.

"Yourself . . . yourself . . ." he repeated.

"And he likes to eat worms and insects and plants," Fudge said at breakfast. "So I'll have to go find him some worms."

"Oh, no!" Mom said. "He'll be very happy eating the food we bought for him at the pet store."

"But Mommy . . ." Fudge said. "You wouldn't feed Tootsie just one kind of food, would you?"

"That's different," Mom said. "Tootsie is a baby. Uncle Feather is a bird."

"I know that!" Fudge said. "But Uncle Feather needs worms to be happy. You want him to be happy, don't you?"

"I'm sure he can be happy without worms!" Mom said, pushing her plate aside.

"Let's talk about this later," Dad said. "It's not the best breakfast conversation."

"Worms, worms, worms, worms . . ." Fudge sang.

"That's enough, Fudge!" Dad said, but Mom was already in the bathroom and she didn't come back to the table.

o   o   o   o

Grandma came to visit the following weekend and was surprised to find that Fudge no longer slept in the hallway outside my parents bedroom.

"I have to sleep in my own room now," Fudge told her. "Uncle Feather needs me."

"Of course he does," Grandma said, standing in

front of Uncle Feather's cage. "And you're a lovely birdie, aren't you?"

"Lovely birdie . . . lovely birdie . . ." Uncle Feather said.

Grandma laughed. "Oh my, and so smart!"

"So smart . . . so smart . . . oh my . . . so smart," Uncle Feather said.

That night, Mom and Dad went out, and Grandma stayed at home with us. We all watched TV together. Tootsie was on Grandma's lap, having her late night bottle.

"So how's kindergarten going?" Grandma asked Fudge.

"I have a nice teacher," he said. "She says I'm as sweet as my name."

"Well, you are, aren't you?" Grandma said.

I snorted.

"Do you think I am?" Fudge asked Grandma.

"I certainly do," Grandma told him.

I snorted again.

"All the time?" Fudge asked.

"Maybe not all the time," Grandma said, "but most of the time."

"Then why do you come here just to play with Tootsie and not me?"

"I come to see all of you," Grandma said, burping Tootsie.

"But you're always holding *her*," Fudge said. "And singing dumb songs to *her*. . . ."

"They're not dumb," I said. "They're from when Grandma was a girl."

"You were a girl?" Fudge asked, trying to get up on Grandma's lap.

"Certainly," Grandma said, shifting Tootsie into her other arm to make room for Fudge.

"You were little . . . like me?"

"Yes," Grandma said. "And I went to school, just like you."

Fudge shoved Tootsie out of the way, so Grandma passed her to me.

"What did you do there?" Fudge asked.

"Oh . . . I sang songs and painted pictures and played games and learned to read."

"You learned to read in kindergarten?"

"Maybe it was first grade," Grandma said, patting Fudge's head. "It was a long time ago. It's hard for me to remember."

"You know what, Grandma?" Fudge said.

"No, what?"

"I'm the middle child now . . . so I need lots of attention."

"Who told you that?" Grandma asked.

"I heard Mommy talking on the phone. It's more important for you to play games with me than with Tootsie. And you should try to remember that."

"What about me?" I asked. "Where do I fit in?"

"You don't need attention," Fudge said. "You're in sixth grade."

I was beginning to get annoyed. "That doesn't mean I don't need attention."

"Everybody needs attention," Grandma said.

"Even you?" Fudge asked.

"Yes, even me," Grandma told him.

"Who gives you attention?" Fudge asked Grandma.

"My family and my friends," Grandma said.

"You should get a bird," Fudge said. "A bird would give you lots of attention. A bird wouldn't care if you were the middle child or not."

"Neither would a dog," I said. "You should get a dog, like Turtle."

As soon as he heard his name, Turtle looked up and barked.

Tootsie opened her eyes and said, "Ga ga goo ga."

"That's right," I told her. "Now go back to sleep."

Grandma went upstairs to tuck Fudge into bed. And I went up to put Tootsie into her crib.

"Good night, sleep tight," Grandma said to Fudge.

"Good night, sleep tight . . . sleep tight, good night," Uncle Feather called.

Grandma dropped the cover over his cage. It's the only way to shut him up. And even then he kept on calling, "Good night, good night . . ." until I kicked the base of his cage.

o   o   o   o

After we'd had Uncle Feather for two weeks, Fudge was ready to bring him to school for Show and Tell. Ms. Ziff invited the other kindergarten class to come and see him, and I got special permission from Mr. Green to skip half of English and go down to Fudge's room in case of an emergency.

Mrs. Hildebrandt's kindergarten class marched in and sat in a circle on the floor, right behind Fudge's class. Uncle Feather's cage stood in the middle of the circle. When everyone was settled, Fudge pulled the cover off the cage and said, "Presenting . . . Uncle Feather!"

"Ooohhh . . ." all the little kids said.

"What a beautiful bird Farley has," Mrs. Hildebrandt said. "Isn't he a beautiful bird, class?"

"Yes," Mrs. Hildebrandt's class answered, sounding like robots.

"Yes, what?" Mrs. Hildebrandt asked.

"Yes, Farley has a beautiful bird," her class said together.

"He speaks French," Fudge said.

"Does he really?" Mrs. Hildebrandt asked.

"Yes," Fudge told her.

"Well, what a coincidence," Mrs. Hildebrandt said. "So do I!" She went right up to Uncle Feather's cage, bent way over, and said, "Parlez-vous Français?"

Uncle Feather cocked his head, looked straight at her and said, "Bonjour, stupid!"

8

Naturally Fortified

"I want to be a ghost for Halloween," Fudge said. "A scary, scary ghost!"

"I think we can arrange that," Mom said. She was feeding Tootsie purple mush from a jar. Tootsie lets half of every spoonful ooze right back out of her mouth, so that Mom has to scrape it off her face and start all over again. It takes three tries to finish off one baby spoonful. Feeding Tootsie can be an all-day project.

"What about you, Peter?" Mom asked. "What do you want to be for Halloween?"

"Sixth graders don't wear costumes," I said.

"Really?" Mom said. "When I was in sixth grade . . ."

"That was a long time ago," I said, interrupting her.

"A hundred years or more?" Fudge asked.

"Not quite," Mom told him.

"What's Tootsie going to be for Halloween?" Fudge asked.

"A baby," I told him.

"Ha ha, Pee-tah," Fudge said, laughing. "You're funny!"

Everytime Fudge laughs, Tootsie laughs, too. And when she laughs with her mouth full, she really makes a mess. So now she had plums all over her face, plums drooling down on to her bib, plums stuck in her hair and plums covering her rattle, which she banged on her tray as she laughed.

Turtle hangs around when Mom is feeding Tootsie. He's developed a taste for baby food. Mom says it isn't good for him. He needs to chew up hard food to exercise his teeth and jaws. And once a week I give him a special tablet to help his breath. Lately he has the worst dog breath! I'm glad Sheila Tubman isn't around to tell me how bad my dog smells, because this time she'd be right.

Fudge says Turtle should rinse twice a day with Precious Breath, this new blue mouthwash that's advertised on TV. Fudge is very big on commercials.

He's memorized all of them, and when we go to the supermarket he drives us up the wall, reciting his dumb jingles about why we should buy this product instead of that one.

My father spends his mornings at the university library and works at home in the afternoons. "How's the book coming?" I asked him one day, when I got home from school.

"Slowly, Peter," he said. "Very slowly. I'm still gathering information. I hope to finish my research by Christmas and start the actual writing after the holidays."

Fudge stood in the doorway, nibbling a piece of cheese. "Dr. Seuss can write a book in an hour," he said.

"How do you know that?" I asked.

"I don't, but I'll bet you he can," Fudge said. " 'One fish, two fish, red fish, blue fish. . . .' 'Do you like green eggs and ham? . . . I do! I like them, Sam-I-am!' "

"Okay, okay . . . that's enough," I said.

"Boys, I'm trying to work now," Dad said. "Do you think you could move to another room?"

o o o o

Later, we were watching the six o'clock news, when Fudge's favorite commercial came on the air. "Oh, look," he said, "it's my dancing cats!" And he put down his Lego bricks and watched.

"Everybody knows that cats can't really dance," I told him. "It's just a lot of fancy camera work."

"Shut up, Pee-tah," he said. Then, he turned to Dad. "They have cat food commercials and dog food commercials and people food commercials, so how come they don't have bird food commercials?"

"That's a good question, Fudge," Dad said, without really answering it.

"Myna birds of the world unite . . ." I began, trying to think up a clever commercial for bird food.

"What's *unite*?" Fudge asked.

"Never mind . . . never mind. . . ."

"You sound like Uncle Feather when you say things twice," Fudge said.

"It's contagious," I told him.

"What's *contagious*?"

"Forget it," I said.

"We should feed Uncle Feather Choco," Fudge said. "If you give it to the one you love, first thing in the morning, you don't have to worry the rest of the day. It has forty-five vitamins."

"No, no," I said. "That's not it. It's fortified with vitamins."

"That's what I said. Forty-five vitamins."

"Not forty-five," I told him. "*Fortified*." And I spelled it for him. "*F-o-r-t-i-f-i-e-d*. It means that vitamins have been added."

"It does?" Fudge asked.

"Yes," I said. "And anyway, you shouldn't believe everything you see on TV, right, Dad?"

"That's right," Dad said.

"You lie when you make up commercials?" Fudge asked.

"No, but we sometimes exaggerate," Dad said.

"What's *exaggerate*?" Fudge asked.

"We embellish to make our point," Dad said.

"What's *embellish*?"

"Sometimes Dad has to stretch the truth," I explained.

"Thank you, Peter," Dad said. "That's a very good way of putting it."

"How do you know so much, Pee-tah?"

"Partly because I'm in sixth grade, and partly because I'm naturally smart," I answered.

"Then how come you got a fifty-eight on your geography test?" Fudge asked.

"Because Mr. Bogner tricked us with matching questions."

"What's matching questions?"

"It's what teachers do to you, to prove you aren't as smart as you think," I said. "You'll find out someday."

"But I am as smart as I think," Fudge said. "So there!"

I wasn't about to get into an argument over that one.

On Friday afternoon, Alex and I were downtown. We stopped off at the movie theater to have a look at the display of *Superman* photos. I had already seen *Superman* in New York, but Alex had missed it, so we decided that when it comes to town we'll try to go and see it together.

Next to the movie theater was an art gallery. There was something familiar about one of the paintings in the window. It was all white, with two black circles in the middle and a red square in the upper left-hand corner.

"I know that painting," I said to Alex.

"It doesn't look like much to know," Alex said.

I snapped my fingers. "That's a Frank Fargo painting."

Alex shrugged. "Who's Frank Fargo?"

"My friend's father. I was over when he was working on it," I said. "Let's go in. . . ."

The only other person in the gallery was a very tall, skinny woman with a neck like a giraffe's and more curly hair than I'd ever seen. She was really good looking. I liked the way she walked, with her head high and her back straight.

"Hello . . . what can I do for you?" she asked us.

"We were wondering about that painting in the window," I said. "The white one with the circles."

"It's called *Anita's Anger*," she said. "And it's by Frank Fargo."

"I told you . . . I told you," I said to Alex, who didn't seem that interested. "I know him," I said to Giraffe Neck. "He's my friend's father."

"Really?" she asked.

"Yes."

"How much does it cost?" Alex asked.

"Two thousand, five hundred dollars," she told him.

"What?" Alex said. "For that?"

"Yes. He's becoming quite famous."

"But it's nothing," Alex argued. "I'll bet I could paint the same thing in an hour."

"Just like Dr. Seuss can write a book in an hour," I muttered.

"What's that got to do with it?" Alex asked.

"Nothing, forget it."

"It may *look* simple," she said, "but I assure you it takes a lot of talent to paint that way."

○ ○ ○ ○

That night I asked my parents if they knew that Frank Fargo was becoming famous.

"Yes," Dad said. "Didn't you?"

"No. Nobody ever told me. Nobody ever tells me anything!"

"Mom and I are considering one of his paintings. It's in a gallery downtown."

"That white thing with the black circles and the red square?" I asked.

"That's the one," Dad said. "Do you like it?"

"I don't know," I said. "It sure does cost a lot."

"That's the problem," Dad said.

"But now that I'm going back to work . . ." Mom began, looking up from her needlepoint.

"You're going where?" I said.

"Back to work," she told me. "I've been offered a part-time job by Dr. Monroe, a dentist in town."

"I thought you were sick of teeth," I said. "I thought you wanted to study art history."

"Art history will have to wait," Mom said. "For now, I've decided to be more practical."

I looked at Dad. *It's because of the book*, I thought. *That stupid book!* "You wouldn't have to be practical if Dad was president of the advertising agency, would you?"

"Peter!" Mom sounded angry. "That's not a very thoughtful thing to say."

I didn't care if she felt angry, because I did, too.

"It's all right, Anne," Dad said. "I think I know what Peter's getting at. He'd like me to be president of the agency. Right, Peter?"

"Well, sure . . . who wouldn't want his father to be president?"

"But I don't want to be president of the agency," Dad said. "And you've got to try to understand that. I do want to write my book, though. And sometimes you've got to do what's really important to you, even if it's not practical."

"And I never said I was sick of teeth," Mom told

me. "I said I wanted to think about a change in careers. So I'm thinking. It will be nice to have a job again. And if Daddy weren't at home, writing his book, I wouldn't be able to leave Tootsie . . . so it's all working out . . . you see?"

"No!" I said. "Everything is different."

"What do you mean?" Dad asked.

"I don't know . . . just everything . . . Mom going back to work, you writing a book, us living here, Tootsie being born . . . Fudge going to kindergarten . . . me in sixth grade . . . everything is different."

"And you don't like it?" Mom asked. "Is that what you're trying to say?"

"I don't know if I do or if I don't."

"Changes take some getting used to," Dad said, "but in the long run they're healthy."

I didn't feel like listening anymore. So I said, "Can I call Jimmy tonight?"

"Sure," Dad said. "Go ahead."

Jimmy answered the phone. "Hey . . . how's it going?" he asked. I could tell that he was eating something.

"I don't know," I told him. "Everything's different. I can't get used to it."

"Well, everything's the same around here, except that you're gone." He must have swallowed because his voice cleared. He told me about school and about our friends and about the way Sheila Tubman is telling the whole world how much she misses me. And then he said, "Peter, I have a confession to make."

"What's that?"

"I've been using your rock. Not just sitting on it, but *using* it. You know what I mean?"

"It's okay," I said. "Don't worry about it."

"No kidding?"

"No."

"You're a great friend. You know that? A really great friend."

"I have a confession to make, too," I said. "I've been using my Kreskin's Crystal. Not just looking at it, but *using* it to get to sleep at night."

"Oh," he said.

"So I guess we're even," I said.

"I guess so." But he didn't sound as if I were the world's greatest friend anymore.

"I saw a painting by your father today," I told him, ready to change the subject. "The white one with the black circles and the red square."

"Oh, that one," he said. "My father painted *that* one right before my mother left for Vermont. One night they had this big fight, and she threw red paint on the canvas. That's how the red square got there. And that's why it's called *Anita's Anger*."

I didn't know what to say, because Jimmy never talks about his parents' divorce. So I changed the subject again. "Do you know how much it costs? Two thousand, five hundred dollars! Can you believe that anybody would pay that much for it?"

"Shows how much you know about art, Peter." It sounded as if he had something in his mouth again. *Pretzels*, I thought. "My father's last three paintings were sold for over two thousand dollars apiece. So before you go around opening your fat mouth, you should find out what you're talking about!" And he hung up.

Great! Just what I needed. My best friend hanging up on me. He'll probably call back in ten minutes, I thought.

But he didn't.

o   o   o   o

I waited until Halloween afternoon to call him. "It's me," I said. "I'm sorry."

"About what?" he asked.

"You know . . . about the price of your father's paintings."

"Oh, that."

"It just so happens that my parents are thinking about buying it."

"Which one?"

"You know . . . *Anita's Anger*."

"Oh, that one. You should tell them to buy a different painting. *Anita's Anger* is a rip-off. Even my father says so."

"But you said . . ."

"I know what I said."

For a minute neither one of us spoke. Finally, I asked, "So what are you doing for Halloween?"

"The usual," he said, "nothing. How about you?"

"I'm taking Fudge trick-or-treating."

"How'd you get roped into that?"

"I volunteered."

"You volunteered?" I think he was chewing gum this time. "You weren't kidding when you said everything's changed!" He *was* chewing gum. I could tell he was blowing a bubble, and I thought I heard the pop when the bubble broke.

My mother and father were surprised when I told them I'd take Fudge trick-or-treating. But Alex said he'd come with me as long as he didn't have to walk next to Fudge, or hold his hand crossing streets, or anything gross like that. Besides, we planned to take him out early, bring him home, then go out by ourselves. And I knew how badly he wanted to go with us, and not with Mom or Dad like all the kindergarten babies.

Alex called for me at six-thirty. And when I saw him, I couldn't believe it! He was wearing a costume. A sheet decorated with black circles and one red square.

"I'm *Anita's Anger*," he said. "You like it?" He turned around a couple of times holding his arms out.

"It's different," I said.

"What are you?" he asked.

"Me?" I said. I was wearing jeans and a flannel shirt, the same clothes I'd worn to school th 'ay.

"He's a sixth grader," Fudge said. "And Tootsie's a baby and Turtle's a dog and Mommy's a mommy and Daddy's a daddy but I'm a scary, scary ghost. . . . Whoooooooooo." Fudge swooped across the room.

"You mean you're not going to wear a costume?" Alex asked. "Not even a mask?"

"Sure I am," I said. "It's uh . . . upstairs. . . . Wait a minute and I'll go get it." I raced up the stairs and found Mom changing Tootsie.

"Where's Fudge's disguise?" I asked her.

She looked blank.

"The one he sent away for . . . you know . . . four cereal box tops and twenty-five cents. . . ."

"Oh, *that* disguise," Mom said, sprinkling baby powder on Tootsie's backside. "I'm not sure."

"But, Mom . . . I need it right away . . . so please try to remember."

"I thought you said you weren't dressing up this year."

"I changed my mind . . . and Alex is downstairs, waiting."

"Let's see," Mom said, fastening Tootsie's clean diaper. "It could be in with Fudgie's toys. He's always liked that disguise. Look in his closet, in the red toy box."

I ran down the hall to Fudge's room and threw

open his closet door. *The red toy box, the red toy box*
. . . let's see . . . here it is! I dragged it out and rum-
maged through it, and there at the very bottom, in a
Pepperidge Farm cookie box, were the black eyeglass
rims attached to the rubber nose, and the stick-on
beard and moustache. I also found an old hat that
once belonged to Grandfather Hatcher. I smoothed it
out and put it on, along with Fudge's disguise. I
checked myself in the bathroom mirror, then ran
downstairs.

"That's mine!" Fudge hollered when he saw me.

"I'm just borrowing it for a few hours. . . ."

"No . . . no . . . no!"

"No?" I said. "Okay . . . then you don't get to go
trick-or-treating with me and Alex. You can go with
Daddy like all the other kindergarten babies. Good-
bye!" I flung off the glasses and rubber nose, tossed
them aside, and acted like I was really going to leave
without him.

"No!" he cried. "Come back, Pee-tah."

"Not unless I get to wear the disguise."

"Okay . . . you can wear it . . . but it's still mine,
right?"

"Yeah, sure. It's still yours." I looked over at Alex,
who was shaking his head. Alex still can't figure out
my family.

We grabbed our UNICEF boxes and our pillow-
cases to hold our loot, and we left.

We worked our way up one side of the street, then

down the other. When we got close to Mrs. Muldour's house, Alex said, "Maybe she'll give us some worms for a treat."

"Worms?" Fudge said.

"Yeah," Alex told him. "She's very big on worms."

"So is Uncle Feather," Fudge said.

"Uncle Feather is a bird," I said.

"Why does everybody keep saying that?" Fudge asked. "I *know* Uncle Feather is a bird." He was quiet for a minute; then he said, "What does she do with her worms?"

"You know. She eats them," Alex said.

"Really?" Fudge asked me.

"We think so," I told him.

We walked up the path to Mrs. Muldour's house, and Alex rang the bell.

"If she gives us worms, we can feed them to Uncle Feather," Fudge whispered.

"Shush . . ." I told him.

Mrs. Muldour opened the door. She was wearing a jogging suit. "Well, well, well . . ." she said. "What a cute little ghost."

"I'm not cute . . . I'm scary!" Fudge told her. "Whoooo. . . ."

Mrs. Muldour clutched at her chest. "Oh my, you are a scary ghost."

"Hi, Mrs. Muldour," Alex said.

"Hello, Alex. That's an unusual costume you're wearing."

"It's called *Anita's Anger*," Alex said. "I got the idea from a painting I saw downtown."

Mrs. Muldour turned away from us and called, "Beverly . . . Beverly . . . come here . . . you've *got* to see this. . . ."

Right away I knew it was *her*. Giraffe Neck. I knew before I could even see her face. I knew by the way she walked from the other room to the front door and by the curly hair. "This is my daughter, Beverly," Mrs. Muldour said to us. Then she turned to Beverly and said, "Alex is dressed as a painting. Can you guess which one?"

Beverly studied Alex for a minute. "Well, with the white background, the black circles and the red square . . . it must be *Anita's Anger*."

"Right," Alex said.

I thought about telling Beverly about the night Jimmy's parents had had their big fight, and how Mrs. Fargo had dumped red paint on Mr. Fargo's canvas, and how Mr. Fargo had named his painting *Anita's Anger* because Anita is Jimmy's mother. I thought about telling her the whole story. But then I remembered how I've told Jimmy things that I wouldn't have told anybody else, and I knew that if I were Jimmy, I wouldn't want my best friend telling the whole world secrets about my family.

"Do you really eat worms?" Fudge asked, out of nowhere.

I gave him a kick but that didn't stop him.

"Pee-tah says you eat them all the time, and he knows everything because he's naturally smart, except for matching questions."

Mrs. Muldour and Beverly looked at each other.

Fudge continued. "So did you?"

"Did we, what?" Mrs. Muldour asked.

"Eat worms for supper tonight?"

Alex let out a groan, and I could see our business going down the drain.

Mrs. Muldour smiled at Fudge. "Yes, we did," she told him.

Beverly added, "There's nothing like home-baked worms. And my mother's recipe is the best."

"We eat them instead of cauliflower," Mrs. Muldour said. "We need to get our vitamins one way or the other."

"Are your worms fortified?" Fudge asked.

Alex groaned again.

"My worms are naturally fortified," Mrs. Muldour said. "They're chock full of vitamins. No preservatives, nothing added. Just the real thing!"

She was beginning to sound like a commercial for worms. I could hear the announcer saying, *"Buy Mrs. Muldour's naturally fortified worms. . . . They're chock full of vitamins . . . grind them up in your favorite recipe, blend them into your milkshakes, serve them instead of cauliflower on those special occasions. . . ."*

"Would you like to taste my special worm cookies?" Mrs. Muldour asked Fudge.

"Yes," Fudge said, following Mrs. Muldour into the house.

We marched through the house to the kitchen. On the counter was a big plate of cookies.

"Fresh out of the oven," Mrs. Muldour said.

"They look like chocolate chips," Fudge said.

"They are," Mrs. Muldour told him. "Chocolate-chip–worm cookies."

"Which part is the worm?" Fudge asked.

Mrs. Muldour laughed. "You can't see the worms. I grind them up and mix them into the flour."

Just like my commercial, I thought.

"Go on," Mrs. Muldour said, offering the plate of cookies to Fudge. "Take one."

Fudge chose a cookie and held it to his lips. But he hesitated and I could see that he wasn't sure he really wanted to taste a chocolate-chip–worm cookie after all.

Beverly took one and shoved it into her mouth all at once. "Ummmmmm," she said. "These are really good, Mother." She took another and ate it quickly, too. Then she brushed the crumbs off her hands.

Fudge bit into his cookie. He chewed it up very slowly. "It's good," he said. "You can't even taste the worms."

Mrs. Muldour offered the plate to Alex and me. We each took a cookie.

Fudge asked if he could have another, and Mrs. Muldour said she'd do better than that. She wrapped a little package of cookies for him to take with him.

When we got home, Fudge dumped out his pillow-case on the dining-room table. He arranged his loot in stacks and counted everything. "Eleven M&M's, seven Nestlé's Crunch . . . five Hershey's without almonds . . . three with . . . two Milky Ways . . . one granola bar . . . four apples . . . and six worm cookies. . . ."

"What did you say?" Mom asked him.

"Nothing, Mom . . ." I told her. "He didn't say anything . . . did you, Fudge?"

"Here, Mommy," Fudge said, "have a cookie. Mrs. Muldour just baked them."

"Thank you," Mom said. She tasted it. "Ummmm . . . very good. I wonder where she got her recipe?"

"It's been in her family for a long time," I said.

"And they're naturally fortified with . . ."

I didn't give him a chance to finish. "No preservatives . . . no additives . . . naturally fortified . . . and chock full of vitamins . . . right, Fudge?"

"Right, Pee-tah," he said, smiling, and I knew that he understood.

9

Superfudge

Fudge has a friend. His name is Daniel. He's pudgy, with a lot of red hair and ears that stick out more than mine. The first time I saw him, he was standing in front of Uncle Feather's cage, lecturing to Fudge.

"Myna birds are native to India and other parts of Asia. The common house myna is a bold, fearless bird, somewhat larger than a robin."

"Robin . . . robin . . ." Uncle Feather repeated.

"Shut up and listen," Fudge told Uncle Feather. "Don't you want to learn about yourself?"

Daniel continued. "The myna is a noisy, sociable bird. . . ."

"I'll say!" I said, from the doorway, where I'd been listening.

Daniel turned around and stared at me. "Who're you?" he asked.

"Peter . . . Fudge's *older* brother," I told him. "Who're you?"

"Daniel Manheim. I'm six. I live at 432 Vine Street. You want to make something of it?"

He delivered the last sentence in a tough-guy voice so that it came out sounding like "Ya wanna make somethin' of it?"

"Not especially," I told him, trying not to laugh.

Daniel turned back to Uncle Feather. "Many myna birds learn to imitate the human voice. They can talk, sing and whistle. The common house myna is genus *Acridotheres*, species *A. tristis.*"

"Daniel is a bird expert," Fudge said.

"So I see," I answered.

"You want to hear about the vulture?" Daniel asked.

"Some other time," I told him.

o o o o

Daniel came for lunch on Saturday. "Would you like peanut butter or tuna fish?" Mom asked him.

"Tuna fish," Daniel said. "You want to make something of it?"

"No," Mom said, looking surprised at Daniel's tough-guy line. "Tuna fish will be just fine."

"Where's the TV?" Daniel asked. "I always watch TV while I'm eating."

"It's in the living room," Fudge said.

"You don't have a TV in the kitchen?" Daniel asked.

"No," Mom said. "We don't."

"I feel sorry for you," Daniel said, pushing back his chair. He stood up. "I guess I'll have my lunch in the living room."

"We don't watch TV while we're eating," Mom said. "So why don't you sit down and wait until lunch is ready?"

Daniel pouted. "I won't have much of an appetite without the TV."

"If you're not hungry, you don't have to eat," Mom said. "TV shouldn't have anything to do with it."

I was thinking that it wouldn't hurt the kid to skip a couple of meals anyway.

"I watch *The Muppet Show*, *Sesame Street*, and *The Electric Company*," Fudge said, as if anybody cared. "And all the commercials. I never miss the commercials. They're my favorites. My father used to write commercials but now he's writing a book. One time I was in a commercial. I rode a Toddle-Bike."

"No you didn't!" Daniel said.

"I did too!" Fudge told him.

"I don't believe you!" Daniel said.

Mom brought the tuna fish sandwiches and two glasses of milk to the table.

"I don't eat anything with onions," Daniel said. "I don't eat lima beans or peas. I only drink chocolate milk, and cut the crust off my bread."

"There are no onions, lima beans or peas in the tuna fish," Mom said. I knew from her voice she was about ready to tell Daniel exactly what he could do with his lunch if he didn't like it. But she walked back to the pantry and brought out the Choco. "You can put in as much as you like," she said, as she cut the crust off Daniel's sandwich. "There . . . now you should be all set."

"Wasn't I in a commercial, Mommy?" Fudge said.

"Yes," Mom said. "Fudge was in the Toddle-Bike commercial."

"See, I told you."

"Did you get paid?" Daniel asked.

"I don't know," Fudge said. "Did I get paid, Mommy?"

"I wasn't there, Fudgie . . . remember? I was visiting Aunt Linda and the new baby in Boston."

"Oh, that's right," Fudge said. So he asked me. "Did I get paid, Pee-tah?"

"You got all the Oreos you could eat," I said.

"I got Oreos," Fudge told Daniel.

"I hate Oreos!" Daniel said.

o   o   o   o

On the same day that Daniel was eating his tuna fish sandwich without onions, peas, lima beans or crust, Tootsie learned to crawl. One minute she was just rocking back and forth on all fours, and the next minute she was moving across the floor. Mom ran to get Dad, and he raced upstairs for the camera. And for the rest of the day we took home movies. Tootsie was the star.

Only Daniel was unimpressed. "All babies crawl," he said.

After a week of crawling, Tootsie became an expert. She could move so fast it was hard to keep up with her. Not only that, but she learned to pull herself up to a standing position. You couldn't leave anything around anymore. Whatever she found went straight into her mouth. And she found everything, from crayons to spools of thread, from Lego bricks to Dad's notebook. She chewed up three pages of his notes one afternoon, and it took Dad all night to try to glue them back together.

Mom and Dad decided to baby-proof the house. They removed everything that Tootsie could possibly reach. Tootsie was very pleased with herself. She said, "Oga, bahfah, fum."

Turtle learned to crawl, too. He'd move across the floor flat on his belly, and Tootsie would chase him, laughing. Turtle and Tootsie were friends.

I kept the door to my room closed at all times. I wasn't taking any chances. Dad put up a gate at the top of the stairs, and another at the bottom.

You had to be careful not to step on Tootsie. She was almost always underfoot. "Put her in the playpen," Fudge wailed one day after she got into his Legos and scattered them.

"She needs the freedom to explore," Dad explained.

"Well, too bad if she gets in *my* way," Fudge said. "She'll just have to learn that I'm her *big* brother!" And clunk, he stepped on her arm and Tootsie screamed.

o   o   o   o

On the following Saturday, Jimmy Fargo came to visit.

"Wow . . . I can't believe how much the baby's grown!" he said when he saw Tootsie racing across the living-room floor. "When you moved, she was about the same size as my cat, and now she's a . . . she's a regular baby."

"Putta . . . Putta . . ." Tootsie said, pulling herself up on my legs.

"What's she saying?" Jimmy asked.

"Nothing . . . just baby talk," I told him.

Jimmy was even more impressed with Uncle Feather than with Tootsie.

"Wow . . . that's some bird," Jimmy said.

"He speaks French. Say *bonjour*," I told Jimmy.

"Bonjour, birdie," Jimmy said.

"Bonjour, stupid," Uncle Feather answered.

I laughed. Jimmy didn't.

"Hey, turkey-brain . . . my name's Jimmy. Can you say that? *Jimmy.*"

"Say that . . . say that . . ."

"No, dumbo! It's *Jimmy!*"

"Dumbo Jimmy . . . dumbo Jimmy . . ."

"No . . . it's just plain Jimmy!"

"Plain Jimmy . . . plain Jimmy . . ."

"I give up, you turkey-brain!"

"Turkey . . . turkey . . . Jimmy turkey . . ."

"Stop it!" Jimmy shouted.

"Stop it . . . stop it. . . ."

"I quit!"

"Quit . . . quit . . . quit . . ."

Jimmy finally laughed. "Some bird!"

Alex came over to meet Jimmy. He said, "So you're the great Jimmy Fargo."

"Who said I was great?" Jimmy asked.

"Well . . . the way Peter's always talking about you . . ."

"Yeah . . . well the way he's always talking about you, I figured you must be the great Alex Santo."

"I am," Alex said.

"Well, then I'm the great Jimmy Fargo."

After that, it was downhill all the way. It's hard to be caught in the middle between your two best friends.

I think Mom knew I was having a hard time, because she said, "How would you boys like to go to the movies this afternoon?"

"What's playing?" Jimmy asked.

"*Superman*," Mom said.

"I already saw it," Jimmy said.

"So did I," I said, "but I wouldn't mind seeing it again."

"I saw it twice," Jimmy said.

"I never even saw it once," Alex said.

"It was better the second time," Jimmy said.

"And I'll bet it will be still better the third time," Mom said.

"Okay," Jimmy said. "I'll go." He bent down to tie his shoelaces.

Mom said, "Wonderful! And the three of you can take Fudge and Daniel."

I had a quick conference with Alex and Jimmy.

"I don't care if Fudge comes with us, as long as I don't have to sit next to him," Jimmy said.

"Same for me," Alex said. "And I won't sit next to the other one either. The other one is a nerd."

"Same for me," Jimmy said.

I went back to Mom. "Okay, we'll take them, but we won't sit next to them."

"That's reasonable," Mom said.

"It's a deal," I told Alex and Jimmy.

We walked into town. We were too early to buy tickets, so we showed Jimmy his father's painting in the window of the gallery.

"I dressed up as *Anita's Anger* for Halloween," Alex

said. "My costume was outstanding, if I say so my-self."

"You don't think you're *too* great, do you?" Jimmy said.

"I'm just telling the truth," Alex said.

"I can't believe this guy," Jimmy whispered to me.

"He's usually not like this," I whispered back.

I never should have gotten the two of them together, I thought. They really couldn't stand each other. And they were making me miserable.

"Hey, let's go in and introduce Jimmy to Beverly," I said, trying to sound cheerful.

Beverly greeted us. "Well, if it isn't Alex and Peter and Fudge!"

"And Daniel Manheim," Daniel said. "I'm six. I live at 432 Vine."

"Glad to meet you, Daniel," Beverly said.

"And this is Jimmy Fargo," I told Beverly. "You know . . . *Fargo*. . . ."

"Frank's son?" Beverly asked.

"That's right."

"I just love your father's paintings," Beverly said. "They're so original."

"He's working on a new one," Jimmy said. "It's called *Salamis on Parade*."

"Sounds fascinating!" Beverly said.

"My father likes salami," Jimmy said. "Salami and onion sandwiches are his favorite."

"I don't eat anything with onions," Daniel said.

"We know," I said.

"Salami and onions," Jimmy said, "my father could just about live on salami and onions!"

Beverly laughed. "I'll bet he doesn't do much kissing."

"That's right," Jimmy said. "My mother's the one who likes kissing. That's why she moved to Vermont."

"Well," Beverly said, "I'd certainly like to meet your father someday."

"Maybe we can arrange that," I said, thinking that Beverly and Mr. Fargo might really like each other.

And Jimmy must have been thinking the same thing, because he said, "He doesn't eat salami and onions every day. On Sundays, he likes lox and eggs."

"I don't eat anything with onions or lima beans or peas," Daniel said. "I hate crust on my bread, and I only drink chocolate milk."

"You're a fussy eater," Beverly said.

"That's right," Daniel said. "You want to make something of it?"

"No," Beverly said. "I certainly don't."

"We have to go now," I said. "We're going to see *Superman*."

"Have a good time," Beverly called.

I wondered if anybody ever went into the gallery besides us. I'd never seen a customer in there.

Outside, a line had formed in front of the movie theater.

As we were walking to the end of it, I spotted Joanne McFadden. She was with Sharon, who's always looking at the ground or the sky, and Elaine, who likes to punch guys in the stomach.

I guess Joanne spotted me too, because she called, "Peter . . ." and waved me over to her. "Give me your money and I'll buy your tickets," she said. "That way you won't have to stand at the end of the line."

Mom had given me enough to treat Alex, Jimmy and Daniel, so I passed the bill to Joanne and stood right behind her. When the wind blew, her hair hit my face, and I didn't move, even though it tickled my nose.

"Well," Elaine said, after we had our tickets, "aren't you going to introduce us to *him*?" She nodded in Jimmy's direction.

"Oh, sure. Jimmy, meet Elaine, Sharon and Joanne."

Jimmy looked at Sharon for a long time. Sharon looked at the sky.

"I'm Daniel Manheim," the little creep said. "I'm six. I live at 432 Vine Street."

"That's nice," Elaine said. "And who are you?" she asked Fudge.

"Fudge Hatcher."

"Your little brother?" Joanne asked me.

"Uh huh."

"I never knew you had such an adorable little brother." Joanne had never said so many words to me at once.

Fudge smiled. "Adorable . . . that's me."

"And I'm Daniel Manheim. I'm six."

"We know," Elaine said.

"You want to make something of it?" Daniel asked in his best tough-guy voice.

"Yeah," Elaine said. "Put 'em up!" She made two fists and held them to Daniel's nose.

Daniel started to cry. "Don't hit me . . . please don't hit me . . . I'm only six. . . ." He covered his face with his hands.

"I'm not going to hit you, you doof!" Elaine said. "I only hit guys my own age. Right, Alex?" And with that, she belted Alex in the gut.

"Cut it out, you . . ." Alex shouted a lot of good words at Elaine.

Daniel jumped up and down, singing, "He said the *A*-word . . . he said the *A*-word. . . ."

"Shut up!" Elaine said to Daniel. "Or I *will* slug you."

"You promised you wouldn't," Daniel whined. "And I'm only six, remember?"

"Why don't you all cut it out," Sharon said, looking at the ground.

We went inside and stopped at the candy counter

to buy popcorn and Cokes. Then we found seats for the kindergarten babies, got them settled, and crossed over to the other side of the theater, where we found an empty row for the six of us. Alex went in first, then Jimmy, then me, then Joanne, Sharon and Elaine. I wondered if Joanne had planned to sit next to me, the same way I had planned to sit next to her.

When the picture started, Joanne offered me some of her popcorn, and when I reached into the carton, our fingers touched. Then I offered her some of mine, so our fingers touched again. By that time my fingers were covered with grease, but who cared? I began to relax, concentrating more on sitting next to Joanne than on the movie, but maybe that was because I'd already seen it.

Then, right when Superman was about to kiss Lois Lane, I felt something icy cold slither down my back, and I let out a yelp.

Fudge was hanging over the back of my seat, with a handful of ice cubes from his Coke. "Hi Pee-tah. . . ."

"You little . . ." But there was no way I could catch him. He was already racing up the aisle.

"Here . . ." Joanne said, handing me a Kleenex.

"Could you do it?" I asked. "I don't think I can reach all the way down my back."

Joanne mopped off my neck and then my back. And when she'd finished, she put her hand close to mine, and the next thing I knew we were holding hands. Hers was soft but cold.

When the movie ended, Joanne, Sharon and Elaine walked home in one direction, and we walked home in the other.

"So what's it like to be in love?" Alex asked me.

"What are you talking about?" I said.

"What are you talking about?" Alex mimicked.

And Jimmy said, "So when's the wedding?"

"Cut it out, will you?" I said.

○ ○ ○ ○

By the time we got home, Alex and Jimmy were talking and laughing as if they'd been best friends for about a hundred years, and I felt left out.

Dad had cooked a big pot of spaghetti, and Daniel was eyeing it until Mom told him how many onions had gone into the sauce. Not only that, but Mom had fixed a bowl of peas as a side dish. And that was funny because we never have anything with spaghetti but bread and salad.

"I don't eat anything with onions. And I don't eat peas either," Daniel said. "What else do you have?"

"Nothing," Mom told him.

"Then I guess I'll go home for supper," Daniel said.

I thought I saw Mom smile.

After supper Alex went home to get his sleeping bag, and he and Jimmy both slept on the floor in my room. I wondered why I didn't feel better about the two of them being friends. Just because they liked each other didn't mean they didn't like me. But I had a hard time convincing myself.

o o o o

For the next week, Fudge walked around talking to himself. "To most people he is Fudge Hatcher, a regular boy. Only his trusty myna bird and his friend, Daniel, know the truth. 'Faster than a speeding bullet; more powerful than a locomotive. . .' "

o o o o

"Do you remember when I was born?" he asked me one morning.

"Yes."

"Did I really grow inside of Mommy?"

"Yes."

"Oh," he said, sounding disappointed.

"Why?"

"Because if I did grow inside of Mommy, then I can't be from another planet."

"Take it from me," I said, "you are definitely from Earth."

A few days later, Daniel told Fudge that he had been adopted as a baby. "So Daniel might be from another planet!" Fudge said.

Yeah, I thought. *That would explain a lot.*

"And he might even be able to fly."

"Don't count on it," I said.

"Daniel is my best friend," Fudge said. "If it turns out he's from another planet, he's going to take me there to visit."

"Swell," I told him. "Don't hurry back."

"You're just jealous because you don't have a friend who can fly."

"I don't even have a friend from another planet," I said.

"Too bad for you, Pee-tah!" And he took off, flapping his arms, and calling, " 'It's a bird . . . it's a plane . . .' "

10

Santa Who?

My father signed up for ten Chinese cooking lessons. He bought a wok, which is a big, round pot, and four cookbooks. Most nights, he would sit in front of the fire, reading.

"When you finish writing your book, maybe you can open a Chinese restaurant," I suggested.

"I don't want to open a restaurant," Dad said, thumbing through *The A to Z of Chinese Cookery*.

"I just mentioned that because Jimmy Fargo's father used to be an actor and now he's a painter, so I thought maybe you were going from advertising to writing to cooking."

"No," Dad answered. "Cooking will be a hobby for me, not a profession."

"Oh," I said. Then I added, "I like to know what's going on, and sometimes you forget to tell me."

"Nothing's going on," Dad said. He flipped through a couple of pages, then turned to Mom. "What do you think about making this for tomorrow night? Stir-fried chicken with green onions, mushrooms, water chestnuts and a touch of ginger?"

"Sounds good to me," Mom said.

"Cocoa and animal crackers sounds good to me," Fudge said. He'd been very quiet tonight, stretched out on the floor with a pad of paper and a fat, green crayon.

"Anyone else for cocoa and animal crackers?" Mom asked, getting out of her favorite chair and yawning.

"Me," I called.

"Make it unanimous," Dad said.

"What's *unanimous*?" Fudge asked.

"It's when everyone agrees," I explained.

"Everyone agrees," Fudge repeated. "That's nice. I like it when everyone agrees."

"What are you so busy drawing?" I asked.

"I'm not drawing . . . I'm writing."

"What are you writing?"

"A letter to Santa."

"Isn't it a little early," I asked, "since we're still eating leftover turkey from Thanksgiving?"

"It's never too early," Fudge said.

"Where'd you hear that one?" I asked.

"From Grandma," he said.

"I thought so."

"That makes it amanimous," Fudge said.

"Hey, Dad," I said, "I wish you'd think twice before you use big words in front of him. Now he's messing up another one."

"Messing . . . messing . . . messing . . ." Fudge babbled.

"It must be pretty hard to write a letter when you can't even write," I said to him, chuckling.

"I can write."

"Since when?"

"Since I was born."

"Very funny!"

"Just because you never see me write doesn't mean that I can't. Right, Dad?"

"Good reasoning, Fudge," Dad said.

"Let me see that letter," I said, suddenly wondering if the kid really did know how to write. *Maybe he is some kind of genius and my parents don't want me to find out because I'm just a regular kid*, I thought. *Maybe they already know that he's going to skip first and second grades. Worse yet, maybe he's going to skip all of elementary and wind up in seventh grade next year, with me. Worse than that, maybe he's going to be one of those kids who goes off to college at twelve. There'll be stories about him in all of the news magazines. And people will say to me, "Hatcher . . . hmmm, that sounds familiar. You aren't, by any chance, related to that child genius, Fudge Hatcher, are you?" And I'll have to admit, "Yeah, he's my little brother." And they'll scratch their heads and say, "Wow . . . too bad some of it didn't rub off on you." Then they'll laugh and walk away.* I reached over and grabbed Fudge's letter. I looked it over carefully. "It's just scribbling," I said, feeling relieved.

"It is not!" Fudge said.

"Santa's never going to be able to read this," I told him.

"He'll read the important part."

"There's only one word that makes sense," I said. *"Bike."*

"That's the important part," Fudge told me, grabbing back his letter.

"I'll help you write a *real* letter," I said.

"This *is* a real letter."

"I'll help you write one to go along with this one, just in case Santa has trouble understanding what you want."

I could see Fudge thinking over my offer. When he's thinking hard, he scrunches up his lips and looks like a monkey.

"Okay," he said. And he passed me the green crayon and a fresh piece of paper. "I'll tell you what to say." He stood over me and began to dictate.

"Dear Santa . . . Please bring me a two-wheeler bicycle. It should be red, just like Pee-tah's."

"Come on," I said, "be original. Ask for a blue bike, or a yellow one."

"Red," he repeated, *"just like Pee-tah's. And no training wheels. Training wheels are for babies."* He paused.

"Go on . . ."

"That's all. I'm finished. I can sign my own name." He printed *Fudgie*, in big letters at the bottom of the page.

"Aren't you going to write your last name, too?" I asked.

"No."

"Suppose Santa gets mixed up?"

"He won't."

"How do you know?"

"There aren't that many kids named Fudge. But just in case I'll put an *H* after my name. That way he'll be sure."

Mom came back from the kitchen carrying a tray, and we all spread out on the floor and had cocoa and cookies.

"I'll mail your letter tomorrow," Dad told Fudge.

"Do you know Santa's address?" Fudge asked.

"Yes," Dad said.

"What is it?"

"Uh . . . I can't remember, but I have it in my

file," Dad said, and he and Mom smiled at each other.

○ ○ ○ ○

"Daniel is asking for a bicycle, too," Fudge reported two mornings later. "So we'll be able to ride to school together."

"*If* Santa brings you a bike," I reminded him.

"Why wouldn't he? I'm a good boy. Aren't I a good boy, Mommy?"

I didn't wait for my mother to answer. "There are a lot of kids who can't get what they want even if they *deserve* to get it. There are a lot of kids who . . ,"

"Why can't they get what they want?" Fudge asked.

"Because toys and bicycles cost money!" I said.

"So . . . Santa doesn't have to pay."

"That's not exactly how it works," I said, gulping down my milk.

"Then how does it work?"

"Ask Mom or Dad. They'll tell you." I gathered my books and zipped up my jacket.

"How does it work?" Fudge asked.

"Hurry up, Fudgie," Mom said, avoiding his question, "or you'll be late for school."

○ ○ ○ ○

When I got home that afternoon, I cornered my mother. "I don't think it's a good idea for you to let him go on believing in Santa. He thinks you can get whatever you want by just asking. He doesn't know about people who can't afford to buy presents. You should do something about that. After all, you told him where babies come from. How can a kid who knows where babies come from still believe in Santa?"

"I don't see what one thing has to do with the other," Mom said. "But I do agree that sooner or later he'll have to learn that Santa is just an idea." She sighed. "But for now, he's so enthusiastic and the idea of Santa is so lovely that Daddy and I have decided it can't possibly hurt. So please go along with us for a while, Peter."

"I suppose you're going to tell Tootsie all about Santa too?"

"I suppose so," Mom said.

"Well, I think it's a mistake!" I said. I turned and walked away. I couldn't remember ever having believed in Santa. When I was three I caught my parents stacking presents under the tree. And by the time I was five, I knew exactly where to look for the presents my parents thought they had carefully hidden from me. And this year I already knew that I'd be getting a pocket calculator from Grandma and a clock-radio from my parents. I heard Mom and Grandma discussing it on the phone last weekend. Sometimes I think it would be more fun to be surprised on Christmas morning. I wish my family would try harder to keep secrets from me.

○　○　○　○

That night, after Tootsie had been put to sleep, Fudge got after the rest of us to write our letters to Santa. "The early bird catches the worm," he said.

"Who told you that, Uncle Feather?" I asked, laughing.

"No, Mrs. Muldour," Fudge answered, seriously. He handed each of us a pencil and a piece of paper. "Only three weeks to go," he said. Then he danced around singing, " 'He's making a list and checking it twice, gonna find out who's naughty and nice, Santa Who is comin' to town.' "

"Santa *Who*?" I said.

"Santa *Claus*!" he laughed, clapping his hands. "Get it? It's a joke. I say Santa Who. Then you say Santa *Who*? Then I say Santa *Claus* . . . get it?"

"Yeah, sure . . . I get it."

"Isn't that a good joke?"

"Yeah, great."

"Daniel taught it to me."

"I'm not surprised."

Fudge put his hands on his hips. "Now hurry up and write your letters to Santa," he said.

Rather than argue, we wrote our letters. I knew what was coming next.

"Now everybody reads their letter out loud. You first, Pee-tah."

I looked over at Mom and Dad. They nodded their heads, encouraging me. So I read my letter, feeling like a kindergarten baby for the first time in a long time.

Dear Santa,
Please bring me one or more of the following items. A clock-radio, a pocket calculator, a stereo for my room, six albums, and a radio-controlled model airplane.
Thank you very much.

Sincerely,
Peter W. Hatcher

"How will Santa know which six albums?" Fudge asked.

"He can just leave me a gift certificate. That way he won't have to waste time trying to figure it out."

"Oh. I didn't know Santa could leave gift certificates."

"Santa can leave anything he feels like leaving," I said.

Fudge accepted that and said, "Now you, Mommy."

When Mom and Dad had finished reading their letters to Santa, Fudge said, "What about Grandma?"

"I'm sure she's making her list," Mom said.

"What about Tootsie?"

"Tootsie's too young to write to Santa," I said.

"Then you write for her," Fudge said, shoving another piece of paper at me.

"Do I have to do this?" I asked.

"It would be nice, Peter," Mom told me.

"All right. *Dear Santa, Please bring me a teddy bear and a pull toy and a . . . a . . .*"

"A box of zwieback," Fudge said. "And that's enough for her. She's just a baby. She doesn't know anything." Fudge was quiet for a minute. Then he said, "What about Turtle?"

"Oh, come on . . . this is getting ridiculous," I said. "And I have homework."

But he'd ripped another piece of paper from his pad.

Dear Santa, I wrote. *Please bring me a rubber ball, some dog biscuits and a new collar. Yours truly, Turtle Hatcher.* I folded the letter, handed it to Fudge and said, "I'm *not* going to write one for Uncle Feather."

Fudge laughed. "Uncle Feather can write his own."

o   o   o   o

Daniel came over the next afternoon.

"Did you write to Santa yet?" I asked.

"I'm Jewish," Daniel said. "I don't believe in that stuff."

"Oh. I thought Fudge said you'd asked for a bicycle for Christmas."

"I celebrate Hanukkah. And I did ask for a bicycle."

"Who'd you ask?"

"My mother and father. Who do you think?"

"I thought maybe you had a Hanukkah Fairy or something."

"You're really stupid," Daniel said, shoving a handful of pretzels into his mouth.

"Thanks, Daniel. Coming from you, that's a compliment."

"You're welcome," Daniel said. Then he walked away mumbling, "Hanukkah Fairy."

o   o   o   o

Our class had a holiday party on the day before vacation, with Christmas cookies and Island Punch. I didn't drink any of it this time, not even one cup, even though I was thirsty. No point in taking chances. We each got to pull a silly present out of a grab bag. I got a pair of red plastic lips. Mr. Bogner brought in a sprig of mistletoe and asked us what we knew about it. Alex raised his hand and said, "If you get caught standing under it, you might get kissed."

"Anything else?" Mr. Bogner asked.

Elaine said, "If you *want* to get kissed you should *try* standing under it."

Everybody laughed.

"Anything else that isn't related to kissing?" Mr. Bogner asked.

No one answered.

"Well, then . . . I think you should know that

133

mistletoe is a plant which grows as a parasite on the trunks of trees. Birds eat the shiny white fruits called berries, but these berries are poisonous to man. Early European peoples used mistletoe as a ceremonial plant. That probably explains why we tend to use it at Christmastime." While he was talking he walked to the back of the room and hung the sprig of mistletoe near the coat closet.

Later, when the bell rang and I ran to get my coat, I found myself standing next to Joanne, under the mistletoe. We looked at each other; then she leaned over and kissed my face, way back, near my ear. As soon as she did, she turned bright red, and for a minute I thought she was going to cry. But she didn't. So then I gave her a kiss, in the same spot, only she moved her head at the last second, and I wound up with a mouthful of her hair.

o o o o

On Christmas morning, Fudge woke the rest of us before six o'clock. "I got it . . . I got it . . . I got it!" he shrieked. "A big, red bicycle without training wheels. Thank you . . . thank you . . . thank you, Santa . . . wherever you are!"

We all ran downstairs to open our presents. Turtle got everything on his list, and so did Tootsie, but she preferred the wrapping paper and ribbons to anything else. Besides my calculator and clock-radio, I also got a surprise—a gift certificate for two albums!

At seven-thirty, Mom whipped up a batch of pancakes. At ten o'clock, Dad fell asleep on the living-room sofa, and Mom conked out right on the floor.

o   o   o   o

That night Fudge came to my room. I was sitting up in bed, reading the instruction manual that came with my clock-radio.

"Will you teach me to ride my bicycle?" he asked.

"Sure," I told him, "As soon as the snow melts."

"Daniel says he's going to learn to ride on the grass."

"That's crazy!"

"If you fall off your bike in the street, you can get hurt," Fudge said.

"So you'll get a few scraped knees."

"Scraped knees bleed, don't they?"

"Sometimes," I said.

"I don't like to bleed."

"Don't worry."

"Did you get scraped knees when you were learning to ride?"

"A couple of times," I said. "You don't fall that much . . . believe me."

"I believe you." He climbed up on my bed and lay back against the pillow. "Santa didn't bring you everything you wanted, did he?"

"I didn't expect him to."

"I would have got you a stereo, but I didn't have that much money."

"I didn't expect a stereo. I was just kidding around."

"Me, too," Fudge said.

"What do you mean?" I asked.

"All that Santa stuff. . . ."

I put down my instruction manual and looked at him. "What do you mean, *all that Santa stuff*?"

"I know there's no Santa," he said.

"Since when do you know?"

"Since always."

"You don't believe in Santa?" I asked.

He laughed. "No . . . not ever!"

"Then why . . ."

"Because Mommy and Daddy think I believe in him . . . so I pretend."

"You pretend? You mean that all those letters . . . and all that . . ."

He smiled at me. "Aren't I a great pretender?"

"Yeah," I said. "You're the best."

11

Catastrophes

Dad stopped talking about his book. I had the feeling it wasn't going very well. Instead, he talked about growing vegetables and how to cook them Chinese-style, or about the Princeton University hockey team. He took me to all their home games. When Jimmy Fargo came to visit, he joined us.

"I'm really into violence," Jimmy said. "I think hockey's a great game. It's a lot bloodier than football, and there are more team fights."

"That's *not* what hockey is all about," Dad argued. "It's a game of skill, of timing, of precision."

"Yeah, sure," Jimmy said. "I know all of that. But it's still great to see the blood bounce on the ice."

"Blood bounces on ice?" I asked.

"Yeah," Jimmy said, "and so does vomit. See, it has to do with the temperature of the ice versus the temperature of the body and . . ."

"Jimmy, please!" Dad said, turning green.

"It's true, Mr. Hatcher. They both bounce on ice."

"Maybe so," Dad said, "but that's not the reason we go to the games."

"I know," Jimmy said. "But it's a nice side event."

Dad shook his head and began to check off players' names on the list inside his program.

Jimmy leaned across me and tapped Dad's arm. "I'm not a violent person, Mr. Hatcher. Don't get the wrong idea. It's just that it's a healthy way to use up some of my aggressive energy."

"Hey, Jimmy . . ." I said.

"Yeah?"

"Shut up!"

"Okay . . . sure," Jimmy said, and he was quiet until nearly the end of the third period when four of the players got into a fight. Then he stood up and yelled, "Kill . . . kill . . " I tugged at his sweater until he sat down again.

Later, when I was in bed and Jimmy was in his sleeping bag, he said, "I've been seeing the school psychologist twice a week. She says I have a lot of anger because my parents split up. Take my word for it, Peter . . . divorce is a catastrophe! You should watch your parents all the time and listen to every word they say, so they can't ever take you by surprise."

For the next couple of weeks I paid close attention to my parents, looking for possible signs of divorce. But I didn't see or hear anything unusual, and soon I got tired of watching and listening. Besides, whenever my parents fight, they wind up laughing.

○ ○ ○ ○

In February, we celebrated Tootsie's first birthday. She carried on a family tradition of smashing her fist into her birthday cake. Grandma, who believes in handing out gifts for everyone, *not* just the birthday person, brought me a four-color ball-point pen, and Fudge, a new Brian Tumkin book.

"Read!" Fudge told Grandma.

She took him on her lap and read him the latest story about Uriah, one of Brian Tumkin's characters.

"I used to really like his books when I was a little kid," I said.

"I'm not a little kid," Fudge reminded me. "Next year I'll be in first grade. You want to see a little kid, look at the birthday girl!"

The birthday girl was sitting in her high chair making a mess. Grandma had brought her a new baby-proof cup, one that refused to turn over no matter how hard Tootsie tried. Finally Tootsie screeched, picked up the cup and dumped her milk over her head.

"Tootsie's first birthday party could go down as a real catastrophe," I said.

"What's a *castradophie*?" Fudge asked.

"It's when something goes wrong," I said.

"Or when *everything* goes wrong," Mom added.

o   o   o   o

Talk about catastrophes! Six weeks later Tootsie learned to walk. At first it was just a few feet at a time, from Mom to Dad, or from me to Fudge. But pretty soon she was toddling all over the place. Sometimes she'd crash-land. And if no one was watching, she'd laugh and start all over again. But if she caught one of us looking at her, she'd start bawling and wouldn't stop until she got an arrowroot cookie.

And Tootsie wasn't the only one crash-landing. Fudge was learning to ride his bicycle. One of his major problems was stopping. Instead of using his brakes, he kept trying to jump off while his bike was still going. I was wrong when I told him he might get a couple of scraped knees. Elbows, knees, and head were more like it. Constantly. But he refused to give up. He was really determined to get to ride to school.

o   o   o   o

Finally, toward the end of April, Mom and Dad decided that Fudge had mastered the art of bike riding well enough to ride to school with Daniel, who had learned on his front lawn, just the way he said he would, without a bruise or a scrape anywhere. And it would have turned out okay, if only Fudge had remembered to use his brakes when he got to the bike rack at school. But he didn't. So he crashed into the rack, knocking down a pile of bikes, and he wound up with scraped elbows, scraped knees and torn jeans.

"Don't tell Mommy," Fudge said, "or she'll never let me ride to school again."

"I think Mommy's going to notice anyway," I said. "You're a mess!"

I carried him into the nurse's room. Miss Elliot washed off his cuts and bruises with peroxide, and when she did, Fudge let out a howl. Not that I blamed him. I could practically feel the sting myself.

But Fudge didn't stop with one howl. He kept it up, making such a racket that Mr. Green, the principal, heard him and came running down the hall.

"What's going on here?" Mr. Green said.

"Scraped knees and elbows," Miss Elliot said.

"Scraped knees and elbows," Mr. Green repeated. "When I was a boy I had scraped knees and elbows all the time. Used to roller-skate and fall down week after week."

Fudge sniffled and said, "Too bad you weren't any good at it."

"Who says I wasn't any good at it?" Mr. Green asked.

"You just said you were always falling down," Fudge said.

"That's because I took a lot of chances," Mr. Green said. "Now, I want you to hurry back to your classroom, because we're having a surprise visitor in a little while."

"Who is it?" Fudge asked.

"It's a very famous man. Someone who writes and illustrates children's books. His name is Brian Tumkin."

"Brian Tumkin is alive?" Fudge asked.

"Alive and well and on his way to our school."

"Brian Tumkin is alive!" Fudge said again. "I never knew that. Did you know that, Pee-tah?"

"I never thought about it," I said.

Mr. Green faced Miss Elliot and said, "Lucky break for all of us that he's agreed to do a program for our girls and boys."

"I'm afraid I don't know who he is," Miss Elliot said.

"Then you must be dumber than I thought," Fudge told her. "First you put peroxide on my cuts, without blowing to take away the sting. And now you don't know who Brian Tumkin is."

"I never blow on cuts," Miss Elliot said. "You can spread germs that way."

"Mommy always blows when she puts on peroxide."

"Yes . . . well . . ." Mr. Green said. "Let's get

back to our classrooms now. It's almost time for our special program."

○ ○ ○ ○

At ten o'clock we all filed into the auditorium. Then, Mrs. Morgan, the librarian, introduced Brian Tumkin, telling us that millions of kids have read and loved his books, and how lucky we were that he was able to make a last-minute stop at our school.

Brian Tumkin walked on stage. He was tall, with gray hair and a gray beard. He waved to us. Then he turned and beckoned to someone backstage. "I've brought a friend with me," he said. "Come on, Uriah . . . hurry up . . . the boys and girls are waiting for you."

Nobody came out on stage, but Brian Tumkin pretended that Uriah had. He pretended to be holding Uriah's hand, and he kept talking to him as if he were really there. I thought, *Either this guy is really whacko or he's a great actor*. Finally he looked out at the audience and asked if any of us saw Uriah. Someone down front called out, "I see him!" I didn't even have to look. I knew who that voice belonged to.

"You see," Brian Tumkin told the rest of us. "One of you can see Uriah. Come on up here, young man."

Next thing I knew, Fudge was on stage. I slid down in my seat.

"What's your name, young man?"

"Fudge."

"That's an unusual name," Brian Tumkin said.

"I know it," Fudge said.

"How would you feel about helping me out today, Fudge?"

"It's a real privilege," Fudge said.

I couldn't believe it! He'd finally learned how to use the word. You could see that Brian Tumkin was impressed. He said, "Well, it's a real privilege for me, too."

"That makes it unanimous!" Fudge said.

"My, you certainly have an impressive vocabulary," Brian Tumkin said.

"I learn a lot of words at home."

"That's wonderful."

"Some of them I'm not allowed to say in school. Some of them my bird can say. His name is Uncle Feather."

I slid lower down in my seat.

"What grade are you in, Fudge?" Brian Tumkin asked.

"Kindergarten."

"Who is your teacher?"

"I started out in Rat Face's class but now I'm in Ms. Ziff's class. She's a lot nicer than Rat Face."

I covered my face with my hands.

"Uh . . . let's get on with our chalk talk now, shall we?" Brian Tumkin said.

"What's a chalk talk?" Fudge asked.

"I'm going to sit down at my easel," Brian Tumkin said, walking across the stage. "And you're going to describe a person to me. And I'm going to draw the person you describe. Do you think you can do that?"

"Yes," Fudge said. "It's a man."

"Oh, I'll need more help than that," Brian Tumkin said, picking up a piece of chalk. "Is he tall or short?"

"He's tall," Fudge said, "and he's got a fat belly that hangs over his pants, and he's mostly bald but he's got some hair around the edges, and he wears glasses, and he's got a pointy nose and a moustache that curls down around his mouth . . ."

Brian Tumkin was drawing as fast as Fudge was talking.

". . . and he's got a crooked front tooth, and his feet are very long, and he walks like this," Fudge said, giving us a demonstration.

"Like a duck?" Brian Tumkin asked.

"Yes," Fudge said. All of a sudden I knew who Fudge was describing, and I wanted to get out of the auditorium as fast as I could. But then Fudge looked out at the audience and called, "Where are you, Pee-tah? I can't see you." And I knew that I couldn't get up without having everybody look at me, so I slouched down as low as I could and didn't answer. "Pee-tah . . . can you see me?"

I let out a groan. Joanne, who was sitting behind me, giggled.

"I can't find my brother," Fudge told Brian Tumkin.

"You'll find him later," Brian Tumkin said. "Now

. . . you haven't told me what this man is wearing."

"Oh," Fudge said. "He's wearing a blue shirt, and a tie with stripes, and brown pants and brown socks and brown shoes and brown shoelaces."

"Brown shoelaces," Brian Tumkin repeated. "Okay . . . there we are. . . ." He brushed off his hands and held up the picture. "Does he look like anyone you know, Fudge?"

"Yes," Fudge said.

"Who?" Brian Tumkin asked.

"Mr. Green," Fudge said.

The audience laughed.

Brian Tumkin smiled. "Who is Mr. Green?"

"The principal," Fudge said.

Now the audience roared.

"Oh dear," Brian Tumkin said. "Oh my." He put his hand to his mouth, and you could see that he was trying hard not to laugh.

Mr. Green went up on the stage then and introduced himself to Brian Tumkin. They shook hands. Mr. Green said, "I think that's a wonderful drawing and I'd like to have it for my office. Would you sign it for me?"

"Certainly," Brian Tumkin said. "I'm very glad you like it." He signed his name across the drawing and handed it to Mr. Green.

Everyone clapped.

Then Fudge said, "Mr. Green, was this a catastrophe?"

And Mr. Green laughed and said, "Not quite, Fudge. But I'm sure you'll try harder next time."

I was sure, too.

12

Tootsie Speaks Out.

One morning in May, Fudge woke me. "Hurry up," he said. "You're going to be late for school."

"Go away," I mumbled.

But he pulled off my blanket and shook me. "You're *really* going to be late for school."

I looked at my clock-radio. Ten after eight. *How come my alarm didn't go off?* I wondered as I jumped out of bed. I raced into the bathroom, splashed cold water on my face, threw on some clothes and headed downstairs. It was quiet in the kitchen. "Where is everyone?" I asked.

"Ha ha," Fudge sang, jumping up and down. "Ha ha

ha . . . it's Saturday! I really fooled you, didn't I?"

"You little . . ." But he was out the back door and running before I could get my hands on him.

I clunked back upstairs and got into bed. *I'm going to kill that kid*, I told myself. *I'm going to tear him to little pieces. I'm going to . . .* I tossed and turned, but it was no use. I couldn't get back to sleep. I heard Tootsie babbling. I got up and walked down the hall to her room. She was sitting up in her crib, flinging out toys, one at a time. She stood up when she saw me, and held out her arms. I lifted her out of her crib.

"Yuck!" I said. "You're smelly." I set her down on her table and changed her diaper. "Yuck!" I said again. The worst thing about babies is diapers. I cleaned her up and dumped plenty of baby powder on her backside.

"Yuck," Tootsie said.

"That's right," I told her. "Yuck."

I carried her down to the kitchen, put her in her high chair, and gave her a bowl of dry cereal to nibble.

Fudge peeked in the back door. As soon as he saw me, he took off again, but this time I chased him. When I caught him I turned him upside down, tossed him over my shoulder and carried him back to the house.

"I'll scream!" he said.

"You do and you're dead," I told him.

"If you hurt me, I'll tell," he said.

"Go ahead and tell." I kicked open the kitchen door.

When Tootsie saw Fudge upside-down, she clapped her hands and laughed. By then Fudge's face had turned dark red.

"Put me down . . . put me down . . ." Fudge cried.

"Never!" I said.

"It was just a joke," he whined. "Can't you even take a joke?"

"Some joke!"

Fudge kicked and hollered, "Put me dooooown!"

"Say *please*," I told him.

"Please."

"Please, what?" I asked.

"Please put me down!"

"Say you'll never wake me up on a Saturday morning again."

"I'll never wake you up on a Saturday morning again."

"Or a Sunday," I added.

"Or a Sunday," he repeated.

"Or a holiday," I said.

"Or a holiday."

"Tell me how sorry you are that you did it today," I said.

"I'm sorry."

"*How* sorry?"

"Very sorry."

"Very, *very* sorry?" I asked.

"Yes. Very, very, *very* sorry!"

I stood him up and watched as the blood drained from his face and his color changed from bright purple to flesh.

"Ha ha," he said, wriggling away from me. "I had my fingers crossed behind my back the whole time. So ha ha ha, none of what I just said is true!" He dashed out the back door again.

I shook my head.

"Yuck," Tootsie said. And then she tossed her bowl of dry cereal to the floor.

o　o　o　o

"How come you're up so early, Peter?" Mom asked an hour later, as she pulled her robe around her and yawned.

"It's a long story," I said.

"Well, it certainly is a beautiful day. No point in wasting it." She poured a cup of milk for Tootsie. "Where's Fudgie?"

"Outside, with Turtle," I said.

"He's such an early bird," Mom said.

"The early bird catches the worm."

Mom nodded and made herself a cup of coffee.

I went over to Alex's house. "Let's do something exciting today," I said.

"Like what?" Alex asked.

"That's the problem," I said. "I don't know."

"We could dig worms for Mrs. Muldour," Alex suggested.

"No, it's too early for worms. I told her the fattest ones aren't ready until late summer."

"Well then . . . what?"

"We have to think," I said.

We sat on the sofa watching stupid Saturday-morning cartoons for the next hour. I got an idea in the middle of *Spider-Man*. "How about a picnic?" I said. "It's a perfect day for a picnic."

"Where would we have it?" Alex asked.

"I don't know."

Alex scratched his head. "How about the lake? We could watch the university crew rowing while we have lunch."

"Yeah . . . that's a good idea," I said. "What have you got to eat?"

"Probably nothing," Alex said. We both went into the kitchen. "My mother shops on Saturday afternoons." He opened the refrigerator. "I was right," he said, slamming the door. "Nothing."

"My father shops on Fridays," I said. "Let's go see what we have."

At my house we found cold chicken, tomatoes, rye bread, fresh fruits and frozen lemonade.

"Great!" Alex said. "Let's pack up."

I went to work making sandwiches, while Alex fixed a thermos of lemonade.

"Don't forget the salt," Alex said.

"Right . . . and the mayonnaise," I added.

"You can't bring mayonnaise on a picnic," Alex said.

"Why not?"

"It's too gooey. And besides, it can make you sick."

"Says who?"

"My mother once got food poisoning from eating potato salad on a camping trip," Alex said.

"But we're not taking potato salad."

"It was the mayonnaise *in* the potato salad that did it," Alex said.

"But we're not going camping," I argued. "We're just going to the lake."

"I don't want any mayonnaise on my food," Alex said. "None!"

"Okay . . . fine," I told him, and I spread mayonnaise on my two pieces of bread.

"And don't forget the salt."

I took the saltshaker out of the lunch bag, held it up, and just to make my point, sprinkled some of it onto Alex's head.

"Very funny," he said, shaking it off.

The screen door slammed. It was Fudge and Turtle. Turtle dove into his water dish and started slurping.

Fudge looked around. "What are you doing?"

"What does it look like we're doing?" I said.

"Making lunch," Fudge said.

"That's right. We're going on a picnic."

"We are?" Fudge asked.

"Not *we*," I told him. "Us. Me and Alex."

"Where are you going for the picnic?"

"The lake."

"I'll come too."

"Oh, no you won't!" I said.

"Why not?" he asked.

"Because you're not invited . . . that's why."

"But I like picnics. And I like the lake."

"Too bad."

"And I said I was sorry . . . remember?"

"Yeah," I said. "And you also told me you had your fingers crossed behind your back, so everything you said was a lie."

"That was a joke," Fudge said. "I didn't *really* have them crossed."

"You know what happens to kids who lie?" I asked.

"No, what?"

"You'll find out." I shoved him out of the way.

He ran out back calling, "Mommy . . . Mommy . . . please can I go to the lake with Pee-tah?"

"No," Mom said.

"Why not?"

"Because it's too far . . . there's a lot of traffic on that road."

Fudge stomped his feet and yelled, "I want to go to the lake! I want to go on a picnic, too!" When he saw us come outside with our lunch bags, he raced toward

me and attached himself to my leg. "Take me . . .
take me . . . take me . . ." he begged.

"Get lost!" I said, kicking my leg free. "Call Daniel.
Count ladybugs. Do something. . . ."

Fudge covered his ears with his hands, opened his
mouth and screamed.

"He's going to wind up with a sore throat," Alex
said.

"Come on," I said, "let's get out of here."

We hopped on our bikes and coasted down the
driveway. Fudge picked up a couple of rocks and
hurled them at us, but he missed. We could still hear
him screaming two blocks away.

o o o o

Alex had to be home for his piano lesson at three-
thirty. And by then we'd seen enough of the crew
rowing, and more than enough of the bugs down by
the lake. Mom and Dad were working in the garden
when I rode into the driveway. And Tootsie was
asleep in a lounge chair.

"Did you have a nice picnic?" Mom asked.

"It was fun," I said. "A lot of ants, but fun."

"Don't forget to rinse the thermos," Dad said.

"I won't," I said. "Where's Fudge?"

"I haven't seen him since you left," Dad said.

"He's probably at Daniel's," Mom said. "He was
very angry."

"I noticed."

At four, the phone rang. I answered. It was Daniel's mother. She asked me to tell Daniel it was time to go home. "He's not here," I said.

"Then where is he?" she asked.

"I don't know," I said. "Wait a minute. . . ." I put down the phone, went to the back door and called, "It's Mrs. Manheim . . . she's looking for Daniel."

Mom ran into the house, wiping her hands on her jeans. She picked up the phone. "Mrs. Manheim . . . we thought Fudge was at your house. . . . No, not since eleven-thirty or so. . . . You found what? . . . Oh, no. . . . You don't suppose . . . Yes . . . of course, right away. . . ." She hung up the phone.

"What is it?" Dad asked. He was standing at the door, listening.

"She found Daniel's piggy bank . . . smashed . . . all the money is gone."

Mom zipped upstairs to Fudge's room. Dad and I followed.

"Bonjour," Uncle Feather said.

"Where does he keep that bank Grandma gave him for his birthday?" Mom asked, ignoring Uncle Feather.

"Here it is!" I said, finding it on his shelf. "And it's empty!"

"Bonjour, stupid . . ." Uncle Feather said.

"Oh, shut up!" I told him.

"Shut up yourself . . . yourself . . . yourself."

"How much do you think he had in there?" Mom asked.

"About two, fifty," I said. "He was counting it the other night."

"So between them, they have close to seven dollars," Mom said.

"Seven," Uncle Feather repeated. "Seven . . . seven . . . seven."

"They can't get far on seven dollars," I said.

"Peter, please . . ." Mom said.

A few minutes later, Mrs. Manheim pulled up in a red sports car. She was wearing cutoffs, a T-shirt that said Ski the Bumps, and sneakers with the toes cut out. Her hair was in one long braid that hung down her back.

"We think they might have gone to the lake," Dad told her.

"The lake!" Mrs. Manheim said. "My god . . . Daniel can't swim."

"Neither can Fudge," Mom said.

"Yes, he can," I told her. "He can doggy-paddle."

"Peter, please . . ."

"Anyway, why would they go swimming in the lake?" I asked. "It's too gloopy for swimming."

"Peter, please!" Dad said.

"Please, what?" I finally asked.

"Please be quiet. We're thinking."

"Let's not waste any more time," Mrs. Manheim said. "The sooner we start looking for them, the sooner we might find them."

"Warren," Mom said, "you go with Mrs. Manheim . . . I'll stay here with Peter just in case they try to phone us."

When they'd left, Mom asked me to bring Tootsie inside. She was still sound asleep on the lounge chair. I picked her up and carried her into the house. She opened her eyes and when she saw it was me, she smiled and said, "Yuck."

At five the phone rang. *This is it,* I thought. *It's all over. They've found him, splattered across the road, his bike a mangled mess. Or maybe the Princeton crew has found him. Maybe they've dragged him out of the lake, his face blue and swollen.* I felt a big lump in my throat. *If only I'd let him come on the picnic with me, none of this would have happened. If only I hadn't wanted to kill him when he woke me this morning. Now it was too late.* I pictured the funeral. Fudge and Daniel, side by side, in small white coffins. . . .

"Peter, would you get the phone," Mom said.

I picked up the receiver. "Hello." I almost couldn't get the word out. How was I going to tell Mom if it was bad news?

"Hi Pee-tah!"

"Fudge! Where are you?"

"Guess. . . ."

"The train station?"

"Nope."

"The bus station?"

"Nope."

"The *police* station?"

"Nope. Do you give up?"

"Yes . . . where are you?"

"At Sandy's Bakery."

"What?"

"Sandy's Bakery."

"Down by the highway?"

"Yes."

"You rode all the way to the highway?"

"It was easy."

"Is Daniel with you?"

"Yes."

Mom grabbed the phone out of my hand. "Fudgie, my angel! I'm so glad you're all right! We've been so worried. Don't move . . . not an inch . . . we'll be right down to get you."

We jumped into the car. I arranged Tootsie in her car seat and we took off. We found Dad and Mrs. Manheim driving around by the lake, told them the good news, and they followed us all the way to the traffic circle and the highway.

Fudge and Daniel were standing outside the bakery. They looked very small. Fudge was holding a paper bag with SANDY'S printed on it. Mom parked, jumped out of the car and hugged Fudge. "I'm so glad to see you!"

I felt another, different kind of lump in my throat this time.

"Be careful, Mommy," Fudge said. "You'll squash your brownies."

When we got back to our house, Fudge settled into Mom's favorite chair and said, "We went to the deli next to Sandy's for lunch. We shared a pastrami sandwich."

"We each had three pickles," Daniel added relaxing in Dad's chair. "And a cream soda."

Mom, Dad, and Mrs. Manheim sat in a row, on the sofa, facing the runaways.

"You know that what you did today was wrong," Mom began.

"It was inconsiderate and foolish," Dad said.

"Not to mention *dangerous*," Mom added.

"And stupid!" I said.

"And while we're very glad to see you," Mrs. Manheim said, "we're also very angry!"

"*Very!*" Mom said.

"And you'll have to be punished," Dad said.

Fudge and Daniel looked at each other.

"What do you suggest?" Dad asked them.

"Put us to bed at eight o'clock tonight," Fudge said.

"That doesn't seem appropriate," Mom said.

"Seven o'clock?" Daniel asked, yawning.

"Yes," Mrs. Manheim told him. "Because you're tired. But that's not a suitable punishment."

"Why don't you take away their bicycles for a month?" I suggested, expecting everyone to shout

"Peter please. . . ." Suddenly the room was very quiet.

"No!" Fudge shouted.

"Not fair!" Daniel hollered.

Mom, Dad, and Mrs. Manheim exchanged looks.

"I think that makes a lot of sense," Dad finally said.

"I think so, too," Mrs. Manheim said.

"I agree," Mom said.

I couldn't believe it. They'd finally taken me seriously.

"But how will we get to school?" Fudge asked, pouting.

"You'll walk," Mom told him. "The way you did before you had bicycles."

"But, Mommy," Fudge began, "if you love me . . ."

"It's because I love you," Mom said. "It's because we all love you and care about you. . . ."

Fudge stood up and stomped his feet. "I'm sorry I bought you any brownies!"

o   o   o   o

Dad took their bicycles, chained them together, and set them on a shelf in the garage. "I hope you both learn that you can't run away every time something happens that you don't like."

"Running away doesn't solve anything," Mom said.

"We had a good time," Daniel said, "so ha ha!"

"And a good lunch," Fudge said. "And we showed

you we *are* old enough to ride to the lake! So there!"

"Oh, no you didn't," Dad said. "You showed us you aren't ready for the privilege of riding your bicycles."

Fudge and Daniel looked at each other again. And this time they both started crying.

We ordered a pizza for supper. Daniel stopped crying long enough to remind Mom, "I don't eat anything with peas or onions."

"How could I forget?" Mom said.

○ ○ ○ ○

After Daniel and Mrs. Manheim had gone home, Mom put her new Mozart record on the stereo, and we sat around the living-room table, working on our family picture puzzle. It's a mountain scene at sunset, and so far we've got one corner of it put together.

"Pee-tah ran away one time," Fudge said, chewing on a piece of puzzle.

I took it away from him and said, "I *thought* about running away . . . but I never went through with it." I found a matching piece and snapped it into place.

"And Daddy ran away when he didn't want to work anymore," Fudge said, stacking up the orange pieces.

"What are you talking about?" Dad asked.

"That's why we moved to Princeton, isn't it?" Fudge said.

"No, of course not," Dad told him. "What ever gave you that idea?"

"I figured it out myself," Fudge said.

"Well, that's just not true!" Dad said.

"Then why did we come to Princeton?" Fudge asked.

"For a change," Dad explained.

"That's why I wanted to go to the lake," Fudge said. "For a change."

"Speaking of Princeton . . . and changes," Mom said, polishing off her third brownie, "Millie and George will be back soon, and we have to decide what to do."

"What do you mean?" I said.

"Well, either we have to find another house here, or we have to get ready to move back to the city."

"You mean we have a choice?" I asked. "I always thought we were living in Princeton for the year . . . and that was it."

Tootsie toddled over, reached up, grabbed a handful of sunset pieces, and ran away with them.

"Hey . . . come back with those," I said, chasing her across the room. I handed her a rubber mouse, and she dropped the puzzle pieces.

"I'm not crazy about the idea of commuting," Dad said, "but if the rest of you want to stay in Princeton, I'll do it."

"Commuting?" I asked.

"Yes," Dad said. "I'm going back to work at the agency."

"No more writing?" I asked.

"Not for now," Dad said. "I've found out I'm not very good at it. I may never finish my book."

I knew he wouldn't. But I didn't say so.

"I'm very good at advertising, though," Dad continued. "And I'm anxious to get back to work." He looked at me. "But that doesn't mean I want to be president of the agency, Peter."

"I know . . . I know . . ." I said. "What about you, Mom? What are you going to do?"

"Well . . . with Daddy going back to work at the agency, I'd really like to get started on my art history classes . . . maybe at N.Y.U."

"That's in the city, isn't it?"

"Yes," Mom said. "In Greenwich Village."

"So you *both* want to go back to the city?" I asked.

They touched hands and Mom said, "I guess we do."

"What about you, Peter?" Dad asked. "What do you want to do?"

"I don't know," I said. "I'm used to it here, but I still miss New York."

"I don't remember New York," Fudge said.

"Of course you do," I told him.

"No, I don't," he said. "Can I ride my bike there?"

"In some places," I said. "Like Central Park."

"I remember Central Park," Fudge said.

"And you remember our apartment," I told him. "And the elevator and Henry . . ."

"Oh, that's right. I forgot about Henry and the elevator."

Mom and Dad laughed.

"What about you, Tootsie?" Fudge said. "Where do you want to live . . . Princeton or New York?"

"Yuck!" Tootsie said.

"Did you hear that?" Fudge asked.

"Yuck!" Tootsie said again.

Mom and Dad exchanged surprised looks.

"That's Tootsie's first word," Fudge said. "She wants to live in New York, too!"

"Nu yuck!" Tootsie said.

I realized that I was the only one who knew that Tootsie had been saying *yuck* all day. And I wasn't about to tell them that it had nothing to do with the city.

"That makes it unanimous!" Fudge said.

"What a big word," Mom said.

"I know a lot of big words," Fudge told her. "You'd be surprised at how many big words I know."

"Fudgie," Mom said, "you're just full of surprises."

o   o   o   o

So, we're going back, I thought. *Back to* The Big Apple. *Back to our apartment. Back to Jimmy Fargo and Sheila Tubman and my rock in the park. Back to walking*

Turtle and back to the Pooper-Scooper. But it's worth it. It's all worth it. I picked up Tootsie and swung her around. I couldn't help laughing. And Tootsie laughed too. To some people there's no place like Nu Yuck. And I guess I'm one of them!